A Pattern of Sorts

Other Works by Ian Gouge

Novels and Novellas

The Opposite of Remembering - Coverstory books, 2020
At Maunston Quay - Coverstory books, 2019
An Infinity of Mirrors - Coverstory books, 2018 (2nd ed.)
Losing Moby Dick and Other Stories - Coverstory books, 2017
The Big Frog Theory - Coverstory books, 2018 (2nd ed.)

Short Stories

Degrees of Separation - Coverstory books, 2018
Secrets & Wisdom - Paperback, 2017

Poetry

The Myths of Native Trees - Coverstory books, 2020
First-time Visions of Earth from Space - Coverstory books, 2019
After the Rehearsals - Coverstory books, 2018
Punctuations from History - Coverstory books, 2018
Human Archaeology - KDP, 2017
Collected Poems (1979-2016) - KDP, 2017

Anthologies

Triple Measures - Ian Gouge, K.M.Miller, Tom Furniss, Coverstory books, 2020
Oak Tree Alchemy - Ian Gouge and Others, Coverstory books, 2019
Play for Three Hands - Tom Furniss, Ian Gouge, K.M.Miller, 1981

Ian Gouge

A Pattern of Sorts

First published in paperback format by
Coverstory books, 2020; updated 2023

ISBN 978-1-9162899-2-5 (paperback)

ISBN 978-1-9162899-4-9 (ebook)

The cover image is a photograph taken
on the Ponte Vecchio in Florence by the
author.

www.iangouge.com

www.coverstorybooks.com

A Theory and A Man

Hindsight. The most valuable tool we have for making sense of our place in the world. 'Valuable'? How about unreliable, or fickle, or pernicious? And we would be lost without it? We compile histories within the boundaries of our lives as if sifting through the confusion inside a jigsaw puzzle box to find the straight-edged pieces, fumbling them together to make a pattern of sorts. But even that takes practice. Lots of practice. When benevolent, not only does hindsight help, not only does it allow us to decipher some of the shapes and colours, it can - if we are very lucky - translate connections, mould together fragments of the picture inside that narrow frame to allow vague images to emerge from the jumble. Yet these snapshots are never the whole story; curating them takes time. And time is the currency needed to purchase hindsight. The two exist in a symbiotic relationship. Or a parasitic one.

We say "hindsight is a wonderful thing", failing to recognise we are enslaved by it, failing to see how it weaves a web like a spider, enmeshing us. We are prisoners dependant on the benevolence of our guard. It feeds us, offers us the illusion of security. Paradoxically, it tells us what to do next; it controls our movements, our thoughts. It defines who we are.

Have you ever noticed how many more words seem to be available when we choose to tell our stories from the relative sanctuary gifted to us by being able to look back on them? The past tense is hindsight's greatest reward. Even though we can only exist in the 'now', we live in the past. It is safer that way. We feel protected - though from what we are unable to say. And for our sacrifice - in part as reward and part recompense - hindsight offers us the richness of language, the blessing of a lexicon made available to us to bestow meaning on what we did. Or what we might have done.

When we tell a story in the present, as if it were happening right now, 'in real time', there is a different sense of 'tense'; something that is taut and sparse and unsure. It is a realm where there are fewer words at our disposal, words that are somehow haphazard, deployed as if we were randomly picking pieces from our jigsaw box without regard, not knowing where they might go, nor with which other pieces they could connect. "Here is a piece" you might say, excited and nervous; but there is another voice which whispers "Give it time; look back on it later; then you will know where it fits". It is seductive, this voice, promising certainty, comfort. And all the while it steals time from you with a Magician's sleight-of-hand, its tricks perfected across millennia.

And what about the future? Can you tell a story looking forward into a world where hindsight is banished totally, where there is nothing but expectation and forecast? You gaze into your crystal ball and say "I will do this" and "I will do that", and you become god-like knowing it will rain or that the bus will be on-time. Or late. Control is yours. Totally. But in this world you have even fewer words at your disposal, the same words, over and over again; and the repetition starts to weigh you down. Under such circumstances there are no individual jigsaw pieces to consider; to caress; all you have is the idea of a jigsaw, and that somewhere there could be a picture towards which you might stumble but never arrive.

Where is the comfort in that? We long for certainty, the assurance of an image we can recognise - in part, at least. A picture grounds us, locates us, gives us hope. It tells us we have meaning and purpose. "Look", a voice seems to say, "here you are, in this space, and with these things about you, with this relation and this knowledge". And it is certainty which seduces us, the certainty hindsight offers. I did this; I was there; I saw this; I said that. All of these things frame us, make us. All of these things validate us. It is hindsight's promise and its reward. And in exchange - as if we had any choice - we give it our lives. We barter away our present, our 'now', in exchange for knowing at some point yet to come we will understand where we achieved or failed, won or lost. We become willing slaves to the missed opportunity, the might-have-beens, and 'once upon a time' is like a soundtrack playing on an endless loop, permitting us snatches of tunes, fragments of intros we might once have recognised. All the songs we sing are the same, yet we are content. And language - hindsight's greatest ally - keeps us in our place as we try to tell our story.

There is no 'now', only 'then'.

But this is not a good beginning. You might argue it is an inauspicious way to start, to lay out such a treatise, such a philosophy. It is uncomfortable at the very least. You do not wish to have to consider such complex and nebulous matters. It is not part of the arrangement. All you want is a narrative, a story; something to transport you away from all of 'this'. You want to lose yourself in someone else's reality - even if it is a fiction - and you do not care too much in which tense it is relayed; you are prepared to give it a chance, to allow it the opportunity to take you elsewhere. Escape is part of the pleasure, and you do not wish to be challenged with questions about the constraints from which you need to free yourself.

What is more, you know enough not to believe all that nonsense about hindsight being a blessing, because you know it isn't. And you actually do believe you live in the 'now'; that you have always lived in the 'now'; that you have 20-20 vision when it comes to the jigsaw of your life - thank you very much! - and you don't need to have someone tipping all your pieces out of the box and onto the floor; after all, it has taken a whole lifetime to get the picture as partially complete as it now is.

So you just want the other side of this bargain 'kept up', as they say; to be distracted with someone else's puzzle as they struggle to make sense of it.

But isn't that a little - 'uninvested'? Or at the very least, lacking in balance? 'Out of whack'? Don't you think it would make a little more sense if you made an effort, rather than simply sit back and say "entertain me"? You might get more from the experience if you were engaged, committed, with some 'skin in the game'. You might, for example, take on the role of the prompter, not exactly to steer the narrative - for how can you possibly do that?! - but to be part of the story somehow. A little more in the 'now' of things, rather than simply accepting it all as 'then'. Wouldn't that be more fun? Potentially?

Why don't we try?

Let me give you a man to play with…

How shall we describe him?

Perhaps we shouldn't describe him at all. The first clause of this agreement is not to spoon-feed you. If you are going to work at this you need to make up your own mind. Think of yourself as a detective of sorts, not that this is a 'whodunnit'. And if it were, where would the challenge be if you were given the solution straight off the bat? At this stage perhaps it is enough to say that he's a man, somewhere in his thirties; he has all his limbs intact and his bodily functions are reasonably performant for a man of his age. He looks - ordinary. There are no exceptional physical marks, scars, or blemishes. He does not twitch or stammer. He is just a man. He might - in many respects - be just like you.

But perhaps we should let him speak for himself.

And then you can talk to him.

And perhaps the others too. The ones that are left. The voices that are not missing.

The Room

Let me tell you about my room.

First, dimensions.

Like most rooms it is essentially a rectangle. Or an oblong. I can never remember which. On the narrow side and directly opposite the door there is a shallow bay with sash windows that overlook the garden. If you were to remove all the furniture you could measure the room by pacing from one end to the other or from one side to the other. Is it strange the way we say 'end' when we mean the walls delimiting the longest dimension of a room and 'side' when we mean those at the shortest? (I had never considered that point until now and suppose it doesn't matter as it acts more as a useful waypoint than anything terribly significant.) Standing with your back against the door and with the window directly ahead of you if you were to take strides into the room paces that were slightly longer than you would normally take if out walking - yet not so long as to look totally ridiculous - you would probably need around seven of them to find yourself in the bay itself and hard up against the glass (which by the way I am assured is not glass at all but a super-tough plastic substitute). Then reorienting yourself against one of the side walls - the plain flat one which runs the full length of the room and not the other which boasts at its centre the breast of a blocked-up fireplace with alcoves also shallow on its wings - and once more taking those same steps it is likely that somewhere between five and six of them will find you flush against masonry again with five landing you short and six proving too many even if you were to walk into one of the alcoves.

Given those dimensions you might be justified in concluding that the room has generous proportions - especially considering that even when I stand up straight and reach as high as I can my hands are still at least two feet from the ceiling and I am a little under six feet tall. It is almost a room that belongs in another era or perhaps in a house filled with such rooms - which is just as well because that is exactly its situation. I have stayed on my own and not on my own in pubs and manor house hotels with similarly grand rooms in which you might find four-poster beds and huge oak furniture plush rugs and roaring fires. Of course there are no such embellishments here though the gardens are formal enough and the building itself looks at least from the outside as if it once had the makings of something impressive.

Now you have a sense of scale what about colour fixtures and fittings?

If we leave the room empty for the moment it better allows me to describe the fabric of it. There is a central ceiling rose surrounded by a circle of elaborate plasterwork entirely in-keeping with the ambiance of the room though it is impossible to say without both a ladder and more in-depth technical knowledge whether the plaster is original Victorian or a reproduction something you might source from a decent DIY shop and presumably glue into place. From the rose a single energy-efficient bulb hangs camouflaged by a large white spherical frame a shade totally nondescript and beginning to betray traces of both age and cobweb as if it has been missed by the cleaners or is something they choose to tackle infrequently. Like the skirting board the picture rail which runs around the entirety of the room including into the alcoves and above the door (but obviously not across the window) is painted high-gloss white and because it is a white which has not yet begun to show the yellowness of age you might assume that it has been painted relatively recently. The door is also gloss white and boasts a handle situated above the keyhole and on its back a single coat hook is fixed about five feet from the ground. Although the room would almost certainly have been wallpapered at some point in its past probably with something bold and vibrant which would look out of place today it is now painted a uniform cream colour not magnolia which has a slightly more muted tone but something a shade more positive as if it is important that you should feel good about the blank canvas with which you have been presented.

Other than a small vent close to the skirting board where the open fireplace would once have been the only other blemishes on the room's surfaces are electrical: a single light-switch near the door; an anonymous-looking button set alongside it in a clear plastic casing; and three double wall sockets one in the same wall as the door one in the alcove furthest from the window and one on the opposite wall in the corner nearest the bay. Combined they are situated to offer the most comprehensive power coverage to the room. In no single respect is there anything of note or particular merit in the entire shell as if it has been presented thus in order to cause as little offence as possible. The carpet is devoid of pattern and boasts no depth of pile - perhaps chosen for its more functional attributes - and its pastel shade of blue is only interrupted by an ovoid cream rug near the room's epicentre which seems almost an irrelevance as if it could have been any colour at all and still been acceptable. In one of the alcoves the one nearest the window three shelves are inset beginning about four feet from the floor and separated by a distance equivalent to a reasonably large paperback book.

Furniture?

Beneath the shelves a chest of drawers designed to look as if it is made of solid wood sits snugly in the alcove with perhaps an inch or two spare on either side dead space that is of no real use apart from facilitating the gathering of dust and things that might fall from the drawers' surface or perhaps to collect the odd fragment of veneer should any be chipped from their edges. There are four arranged in three rows two of equal size make up the top row with two full-width drawers beneath these the bottom one being of considerably greater depth than all the others as if it has been specifically designed to contain bulky items which need to be folded away. For clothes that can be hung there is in the other alcove a two-door wardrobe apparently constructed from the same material each of the doors made of three isometric panels slightly inset as if to further enhance an illusion of solidity these doors having been garnished with vaguely garish silver knobs which you can't help but notice are totally out of keeping with the wood-effect and at odds with the more traditional knobs on the aforementioned drawers. All of this leads you to the conclusion that at some point the originals were lost perhaps their threads compromised and that the only spare knobs to-hand were the silver ones now in situ.

Running along the wall opposite the old fireplace a single bed occupies the corner of the room its head hard against the wall with door in it a small bedside table hosting a simple lamp and a clock (battery - it is not ticking) breaking the space between the two. The frame of the bed is also wooden but of a different finish to the wardrobe and chest of drawers and at both first and second glance appears of greater age which might lead you to assume that the bed itself will be uncomfortable but that would be to ignore the quality of the mattress which has only recently been replaced and is of such a subtle firmness so as to ensure a good night's sleep.

But I digress.

In the bay of the window there is a small desk-cum-table not professional enough to be the former nor simple enough to be the latter. You might consider it something of a halfway-house though given it is home to books paper and pens how it is currently being used seems plain enough. The chair which addresses it is high-backed and somewhat austere giving the impression of it being the oldest item of furniture in the room. As with the bed you might assume for this and many other reasons - such as its shape its colour the apparent thinness of the cushion that adorns it - that the chair will be uncomfortable to sit in but you would be wrong.

Between the desk and the end of the bed there is sufficient room for a pair wingback armchairs their faded maroon velour covers not betraying age as much as a lack of quality and unlike the desk chair and the bed although these give the impression that they would be the most comfortable pieces of furniture in the room once again they prove the lie.

With the room now fully furnished and restored I have assumed my normal pose right leg crossed over left arms folded sitting in the armchair nearest the desk it being angled in such a way as to allow me a view out of the window or towards the door with the merest turn of the head in either direction. Having volunteered to provide this brief tour of my room (this guidance if you will) I have been forced into considering the whole once more and find that it is as with so many things familiarity having bred contempt. When I examine it dispassionately I find the flaws in it: the fraying of the rug; the chip from the bed frame; the grooves gouged into one of the legs of the desk-cum-table; the crack in the middle panel of the left-hand wardrobe door; the way the middle drawer sits slightly askew from its neighbours. Needless to say there is no satisfaction in such rediscovery and the only thing that prevents any decline into discontent on my part is the fact that I am not alone that I have a visitor a new person I have not met before. And even though I have been told the reason you are here and even though I do not believe that cock-and-bull story - I know what you want to know! - I am sitting quietly dutifully in my usual place waiting.

The First Interview

And now it is your turn.

Imagine you are sitting in that room, having been directed to the vacant of the two armchairs, and that he is sitting across from you, waiting. He knows you have some questions to ask him. It is a prospect about which he may - or may not - be nervous. It is difficult to tell as he looks at you now, evenly, his gaze impossible to interpret.

Finding the room precisely as he had described it, something in the passage of time to which he has alluded brings to mind notions of 'now' and 'then'. As a result, your first question seems obvious.

"Tell me about something or someone from your past."

My past?

"Yes. Describe it to me. An event, perhaps."

I always find myself searching for words to describe everything I've ever seen or known or felt. Words hiding in the shadows. And all the while memories queue up waiting to be processed wanting to be labelled like that weekend in the strange upside-down house in Salcombe - Anne resplendent - all of us drinking too much wine and playing Charades another game looking for words. I remember an alleyway between buildings walking out the back door of the house down the funny little courtyard garden and through the gate turning right and then being absorbed by the small town by a dark space narrow and overhung leading to where pubs wrote their menus on chalk boards fixed to outside walls to be mutilated by the rain or a passing shoulder or deliberately adjusted their dishes struck off when the pub ran out of scampi or cream trifle. 'The Fortescue Inn'. 'The Salcombe Yawl'. For a few strides we walked hidden in the darkness away from the sun the sound of the sea waves against the harbour wall the slapping of water against the hulls of boats the rapping of tackle against yachts' masts as if they were beating out a rhythm or marking the passing of time.

"Anne?"

Anne is now a composite a collage of out-of-focus virtual snapshots slices of her taken at jaunty angles fragments as she stood looking out at the ships a dog jumping at the breakers the horizon the trace of an arm a cheek a smile all clues to a puzzle I can no longer put together in a comprehensive way betrayed by my memory betrayed by myself. I see her walking ahead of me through that dark tunnel perhaps laughing or pointing to something displayed in the window of a shop its contents designed to trap the unwary tourist weighed down with too much money and I have no idea who she was talking to or what she was saying or what she saw. And later on the cliff path not with the others walking towards an unkept rendezvous somewhere for tea and scones - jam or cream first?! - the wind strong enough to steal words turning voices into a silent endeavour though the gulls were cawing overhead and from somewhere far below the occasional shouts of children at play at the edge of the water kicking balls or throwing stones or building sandcastles only for the sea to later scrub them away.

"Was that where the two of you met?"

She arrived weeks before in a blaze of light opening the front door of a dark pub in my cathedral city as we sat drinking beer and weighing up the merits of the inconsequential and waiting for something to happen. Then there she was pausing on the threshold allowing the backlight from outside to frame her as if she needed a halo to envelop her before she saw us before she waved to Josh walking to where he now stood me sitting beside him he giving her a brief hug Anne smiling as her big brother introduced her to us before he took her away to the bar to buy a drink. And in that brief absence we shuffled making room for another chair me already hoping she would choose to sit next to me because in those few seconds I knew I was already lost and that my future had been irrevocably changed by that image of her shrouded in light by the way she walked the way she smiled. I felt my life's memories being reset in advance as if they were already fixed not waiting to be made but waiting to be replayed me knowing that one day - as if I were a man being slowly swallowed by quicksand - I would eventually cease to struggle and accept my fate. Later would come the search for words the beginning of a search that would never end that would lead to this. It was as if someone had pressed 'restart' on my life a reboot a fresh chance as if everything that had come before had been devalued junk stock worthless. Suddenly cast adrift shipwrecked robbed of everything and praying for salvation I raised my glass again silently excusing myself from the conversation the debate and sipped and waited waiting for them to come back from the bar for Anne to sit down next to me not her brother and for someone to press 'play' on my life so that I could start it over like the first frame in a movie once all the titles have rolled.

It was a way she had generating that first impression as if it were a super-power bestowed upon her a power that could rob you of sense entrap you whole and in your blindness be struck down so that it was impossible to see anything else to conceive of no other reality. Only later was the veil lifted and even then those images remained the perfect romance of them like a baited and barbed hook from which it was impossible to wrestle free and even if you could you would never curse the angler who cast the line believing they had been as innocent as you. I told myself Anne had reserved this power of hers for me alone as if she had been waiting all her life to walk into that pub to sit next to me on that stool to begin our dance with the ostensibly vacuous words "Josh tells me you're the sensitive one" at which everyone laughed me included even though I could feel my skin redden my entire body feeling crimson like a lobster which only made then laugh all the more. Then her hand on my arm an apology impossible not to accept.

"You were at her mercy?"

Are you enthralled or in thrall? Or is it both when subject to a spell that can only be cast by the most powerful of souls and works on only the most susceptible of subjects? Such questions are never asked because the helplessness it infects is total like when she first held my hand at an amateur art exhibition we had stumbled onto in a dilapidated but quaint little hall in a forgotten backstreet of a picturesque coastal village famous for fossils her touch sucking out any remaining resistance I might have thought I had. Not that it mattered all she was trying to do was to get my attention to point out a landscape made from fabric of some kind knitted or crocheted or felted and where instantly to my eyes its sea suddenly looked as wet as it was possible for a sea to be the cliffs dramatically sheer and all because she had approved of them. And when I squeezed in reply gently exploring not in recognition of the picture but to acknowledge the presence of her hand to make a statement as to what she had done to me to offer myself to her without reservation she smiled and allowed her fingers to link with mine as if secretly sealing the pact.

A little later we sat on a warped wooden bench outside a pub drinking bottled lager and watching families with picnics being terrorised by seagulls who had established their own order of things aficionados of fish-and-chips perhaps preferring plaice to haddock or haddock to cod but always any port in a storm and she asked me about my childhood because she had established I had grown up near a coast somewhere one that suddenly seemed a million miles from here even though it wasn't. It was a request to which I was happy to acquiesce not because I was self-centred or narcissistic or proud of my heritage but because it allowed me to apply the glue of history between us to strengthen the bond to demonstrate my newly-found trust and that my history had become suddenly and wonderfully both *our* combined history and *our* combined future as if sharing it was the most natural thing in the world and granting her that privilege would allow her even greater possession of me.

Enthralled or in thrall?

"So what was your childhood like?"

My childhood?

"Humour me."

There was a great deal that was dilapidated in the city where I grew up and virtually nothing that might be regarded as quaint or unique such epithets blown away by the size of the place and the harsh sea breezes that flew in off miles of pebbled beach stones so hard and misshapen that they seemed to dig into your very being when you walked on them barefoot. I remember as a child being traumatised by my experience of the stones the coldness of the winds the bone-aching chill of the water that seemed to suck all the heat from your body stealing it away to be redistributed elsewhere each of us making our own little contribution to currents that ended up being warmer somewhere else. Nothing mitigated the agony. There were never any games or treats sufficient enough to compensate for the dread in advance of the arrival at the beach or once arrived the longing to be wrapped in a large towel at the end of the day and within its unreliable confines slide off trunks freezing fingers struggling for purchase on the damp waistband and all the while in trepidation that the towel would slip uncontrollably or the wind whip it away to reveal my small childish whiteness to the world and allowing everyone to laugh and point. Perhaps even then I became an exile without realising it became nurtured to want to escape to be a slave to the expectation that the next place would always be better than the last and the one after that better still.

"You were - or became - nomadic?"

I had a grounding in mobility. As a family we moved a lot when I was a child each journey to a new house in another part of town like a mini adventure the excitement of a new bedroom of being able to decorate it afresh with paints and pictures to lay out my books in a different order on the bookcase that always travelled with me until the day it just fell apart coming off the back of another removal lorry. Episodic years that were romantic at the time and only lost their sheen as I edged unexpectedly into puberty and all the burgeoning realisations that came with doing so. To that point my life had been something of a Grimm fairy tale my parents spinning yarns to justify why we were moving again stories about my father's work new jobs new opportunities but never the truth not until much later when it really dawned on me realisation triggered as the kids in yet another new school chose to pick on me for something I hadn't done or something beyond my control like the frailty of my worn uniform its hems extended and patched again and again my shoes unredeemable no matter how much polish my mother chose to apply on a Sunday evening.

"But you weren't an only child?"

Mine was an elongated baptism from which Matt was spared arriving as he did not long after my fifth birthday and not long after yet another move this time to a slightly larger house in a slightly worse part of town its proximity to the sea offered as compensation for the lack of any other amenity and the proliferation of Saturday crowds that flooded the streets on their way to and from the nearby football stadium. On certain days when the wind was up and off the sea - so most days it seemed - I could hear the stadium announcer as he boomed the players onto the pitch and with a little practice I was able to tell the score from the noises that came from the terraces from their volume and tone and to make up for never being taken there by my father I used to play a game with myself to see if I had guessed the score correctly when the results were shown on 'Grandstand' at five o'clock. From the very beginning Matt had little impact on me as the gap between us was too great for me to take him seriously. He became an annoyance an encumbrance whose presence often became the reason for us to do things or not do things. In the main it was the latter an outcome which sometimes left me alone to pursue what I chose and live my life largely in the way I wanted. To that extent he proved more of a liberator than anything else although not for my parents who half the time seemed to regard him with suspicion as if he had snuck into the house when they weren't looking or had been left in a shabby basket on the doorstep with a crumpled note begging mercy. Not too many years later their luck turned and we pretty much stopped moving and their attitude towards him seemed to change as if he had suddenly become something of a good-luck charm. When I eventually left home some eleven years later heading inland and away from the drag of the sea he was still trying to catch up in lots of ways never one step behind me but many more than that and no matter how hard he tried to ingratiate himself with me the gulf between us was always too big and at no point during those formative years did I ever really regard him as anything other than a minor nuisance there being no love lost because there was never any love between us to lose. When I was around fourteen I grew suddenly spurting upwards to become taller than my mother and then a year later taller than my father and as if height had anything to do with it they then tried to admonish me for not being a role model for him. But I had no concept at that stage of what a role model was childishly believing that you needed to excel at something to qualify and from what I could see all my experience taught me was that I was good at nothing in particular except playing the role of an only child with my grades at school keeping a low profile and maintaining a stubbornness to never threaten abandonment of the mediocre. Average or not and whether I had been held back or dragged down in my formative years by our continual domestic moves the changes of school the rotation of friendships on ever-shorter cycles somehow I still managed enough mediocrity to qualify for university succumbing to the well-worn drudge of academic pathways even though I had no inking as to what I was doing nor what I really wanted to do afterwards. Perhaps that was one of the first conscious incarnations of my philosophy about the next thing being better than the current thing for I had unconsciously managed to expand that optimistic mantra to apply to more than just where we lived not seeing it as fatalist or passive until a little while later when it was proven more than once that the next experience could be much *worse* than the one before.

"Presumably Anne changed all that."

By the time Anne walked through that pub door my philosophy had been watered down somewhat and given a varnish of cynicism that I preferred to think of as pragmatism or realism or the application of experience gained the hard way even though in my more lucid moments even I could recognise I hadn't experienced anything that was truly tragic or disastrous preferring rather to apply a negative gloss on minor setbacks in order to lend them gravitas and make them more meaningful. My wanderlust had been in hibernation for a while as somewhat ironically university had provided me with a greater degree of domestic stability than I had ever known at home ironic because for the majority of my peers leaving home and setting out on their own gave them the experience in reverse the chance to flit and drift and see where the world took them not to release an anchor and seek the steadfast. It was an upbringing including the parenthetical experience with Matt which Anne shortly after our finger interlocking demanded to know insisting that I should reveal it strictly in chronological sequence with as little as possible left out because she was firmly of the opinion that one thing led to the next in an unbroken causal chain within which not a single moment or experience or action was ever irrelevant. She argued hers was a belief system clearly different to that of a fatalist because fatalists were people who abdicated all responsibility for what happened next allowing their lives to be governed by supposedly superior unseen forces whereas she believed in absolute responsibility based on attaining the highest possible level of self-knowledge and understanding. Once I asked her if that meant she was always working things out calculating next moves based on past ones weighing odds before she made any decision and if so what did that say about her and that moment when she walked into the pub choosing to sit next to me when she came back from the bar and agreeing weeks later to go to Staithes for fossils and chips impromptu art exhibitions and then consented to the holding of hands. She laughed and told me not to be silly.

"What did Matt think of her?"

"So are you going to make this one last?" Matt's question came as we sat in our parents' back garden taking respite from the festivities inside the house an escape in order to allow him to indulge in a cigarette his one idiosyncrasy against a life led on the straight and narrow a nod to difference to being even remotely interesting. We had met again for their thirtieth wedding anniversary coming together as old foes might with an air of truce surrounding us even though there had been no disagreement no fighting involved it being just the way we had an air of mild disinterest as if we were old colleagues professional rivals rather than kith and kin. It was a question which allowed him to occupy the moral high ground after my announcement about Anne - our relationship just a few weeks old so not mature enough to inflict my family on her - had been met more by apathy than anything else although I knew even as I let it slip over tea earlier in the day that he would have something to say on the matter his self-certified qualification for doing so coming from two sources. The first was the longevity of his own relationship having met Stella during their second week at Sussex University and them now nearly five years on still being together a solid couple who seemed to have found a groove from the first moment a groove into which they both dovetailed as if there had never been any question any possibility of an alternative outcome nor of there being any other person in the whole world who would do for either of them. Yet I had always been suspicious that what they enjoyed was somehow sterile more functional than anything else a coupling which lacked passion frisson danger that was never going to go anywhere other than where it was. It seemed to me to represent a destination rather than a journey as if the two of them had already settled - though for exactly what I wasn't sure. In any event it gave Matt the upper hand at least in his own eyes especially when he brought into play the second source for his statement which was the abject failure of any of my previous relationships to achieve the blissful nirvana he claimed to have obtained. It was one of the areas where he tried to assume the role of the older brother as if he were qualified to do so and I was just some pathetic underling who still had much to learn.

"So he had a point?"

On a purely factual level he had some justification as my record at university and subsequent all too infrequently punctuated tracts of emotional sterility had been less than impressive if measured against the tenets he held most sacred which at that time at least were based on longevity stability reliability certainty and confidence. I had either tripped or dived headlong into and out of variously tempestuous or fragile or whirlwind relationships one or two every term or every year with girls who all possessed something I didn't as if I was trying to make up for a personal failing by attaching myself to someone who could compensate for whatever it was I lacked not that I saw it that way at the time. Sue was extrovert gregarious flighty magnetic like a beautiful butterfly I tried to capture in a net I didn't realise was full of holes. One minute she was there and gone the next. Debbie intellectual serious deep profound rigorous in her ability to analyse things which eventually - it didn't take long! - allowed her to see through me and weigh the scope of what I offered her which proved by her calculation to be very little indeed. Liz was passionate intense romantic with all the letters in capitals not just the 'R' but she was really seeking a soul mate a Byron and mistook my early ham-fisted attempts at being a poet as a sign. Ours was the flame that burned brightest but for the shortest amount of time and with the greatest subsequent pain. Sarah was sporty and athletic, Rachel religious and devout. It was as if I was ticking-off types characteristics profiles on a perverse emotional bucket-list to see if I could complete the set before I left university perhaps putting all my eggs into the basket those three years represented in the vain hope that one of them might prove in the end not to be cracked or completely broken. Maybe I was the one who ended up the most scrambled of all. When I met Jenny my first year after college she never stood a chance partly because I had lost all sense of what I was supposed to be looking for and along the way had forsaken any notion of who or how or why I was supposed to be in a relationship with a woman. I think she had been my favourite and the person I hurt the most the one time when I was dealing the shitty cards taking advantage held the upper hand was in control however you want to describe it and I can't help wondering even now if things would have been different if I had met her before all the rest and whether or not I would have ended up more like my baby brother seemingly settled happy content. Yet such an outcome would hardly have fitted my philosophy that the next time will always be better than the last and the one after that better still. It was a philosophy I extended to my girlfriends not consciously but because I had to considering it was the only way I could move on though it wasn't really moving on more like a blind man stumbling along an uneven path or an alcoholic wracked by cold turkey between drinks. If I was an addict by the time I met Jen then what chance did the poor girl have? In any event Matt's question had some justification even though I resented him asking it almost as much as I resented him being in the position in which he felt he *could* ask it. But having done so there was a need for an answer if not for him then for me an answer to a question that perhaps I had known was immediately there from the moment Anne's fingers interlocked with mine but which had been lurking in the shadows out of sight waiting for the right moment to pounce and as it turned out that moment was provided by my inadequate sterile little brother as he smoked his pathetic cigarette outside our parents' back door.

"I don't know," I said. Though now I do. Obviously.

And then he asked me to describe her as if having seen me struggling to engage with him on the playing field where he had obligingly marked out the extremities the boundaries not be be crossed in a game where the unspoken rules were also his doing so was a deliberate twisting of the knife knowing I would as yet be unable to make a decent fist of it me knowing I was uncertain as to how far short I would fall. It was further solid ground for him in that had I asked him to describe Stella he would have been able not only to comply but to do so in the most minute of detail as if he kept a log where he wrote everything down about her all his observations reserved for just such a moment when his profound and intimate knowledge might be called upon. Rightly or wrongly I chose not to back down not to give in or offer him the satisfaction the recognition that in comparison to his comprehensive insight into Stella I hardly knew Anne at all - but more than that it was not until that precise moment I realised I had no true grasp of what I did or did not know about her. "Physically?" I asked buying time to marshal the meagre forces at my disposal to which his reply - "whatever makes you feel comfortable" - merely thrust and twisted the knife deeper the way an assailant does when they know they are in the ascendance and have bested you.

"She's petite really, though not in any sense of being insignificant; a little shorter than average I guess but proportionally perfect. She has wonderful hair. It's very dark, a little longer than shoulder length, but it has this tremendous propensity to look fantastic however she chooses to wear it: up, down, tied back, curled - you name it, she can make it look great. And she takes advantage of it too, using it almost as an extension of her mood. She has crystal clear dark brown eyes set a fraction deeper than what you might regard as the norm I suppose, but all the more penetrating for that - especially when she chooses to apply make-up, which doesn't happen often. And she has wonderful hands, particularly her fingers. There is something elegant about them. They move slowly, deliberately, and I think they are slightly longer than average, so having said she was perfectly proportioned I guess that's not so in all aspects. Apart from that - or maybe with all of that - there's nothing outwardly remarkable about her. She's not the kind of person who would turn heads in a crowd, not immediately anyway; but she has a certain irresistible quality that draws you in. I don't think it's magnetism because that's something else entirely, but she has the ability to captivate, to charm, to make you want to know her and for her to be your friend. What else? She's bright, sharp as a tack; doesn't stand any nonsense, is honest, tells it like it is - but not in a nasty way. And she seems to have the ability to elevate things from out of the ordinary, to promote them to be more than they would be otherwise." I immediately thought of those fabric landscapes. "Yet none of any of that is achieved overtly or proudly; she never makes a fuss or tries to pretend that it's all about her. I don't think she has a self-centred bone in her body. We talk a lot, about normal things and serious things; but she can be flippant and casual too, even silly when she wants to be. She believes passionately in cause and effect, makes me laugh and frown and smile, and so far she hasn't made me cry, not in a bad way. So for all those reasons - and for many more I can't put words to - I think she's good for me; she fits. We fit. I'm happy, which is probably the simplest accolade I can offer on her behalf. And even though I'm okay to be here for mum and dad, I can't help wishing I was somewhere else.

"Does that answer your question?" I asked him.

"And did it?"

Under the circumstances and given the passage of time there can be no surprise that I can't remember Matt's reply especially as I'd been busy both speaking and listening to myself at the same time unravelling my monologue and wanting to see if I could stay outside myself somehow to try and come to a conclusion as to what I thought about what I'd said of her. In the end I wasn't entirely clear whether I'd answered Matt's question to *my* satisfaction never mind his me struggling to decide if the picture I'd painted was accurate yet knowing simultaneously that it had to be entirely *in*adequate that it was impossible to describe Anne because it wasn't how she looked or behaved which singled her out. The tangible was almost irrelevant it was how she made me feel that was the most important thing - and the one thing for which I would certainly have been unable to find the right words. How could I describe in an adequate enough way the first time I saw her or the cliff path walk or the visit to Staithes? Did I have sufficient words to do her justice or be true to what I felt especially as I really had no idea exactly what I was feeling shying away from giving it labels trying not to invite parallels with my history and with what supposed romantic success - usually before inevitable romantic failure - felt like. I could have said "I have no desire to repeat the mistakes of the past" and that might have been the most accurate summary I could have offered that and platitudes about the future about taking one day at a time even making an assertion that I was an entirely different person now was changing daily and had Anne to thank for that. And after all that analysis condensed into no more than a minute or two Matt stubbed out his cigarette on the patio with his right shoe smiled and stood saying "Well then" as if it were the most profound comment in the world.

As I watched him walk away I saw him taking my words with him knowing he would have already lost most of them before he crossed the threshold back into the house leaving them like a trail behind him as if they were unimportant a broken chain of clues from which all he held on to were the few he chose to keep that seemed relevant. If I had followed him and asked him five minutes later to repeat what I had said I wonder what his response would have sounded like how close it might have been to my own description and thus in the retelling become a portrait even further from what Anne was really like. There would have been a gulf. How could it be otherwise? And as if to provide a contrast stark as a yawning chasm I found myself two days later answering Anne's questions about my weekend at my parents and reciprocally about Matt her approach being the complete opposite of my brother's with a focus on specifics giving me no room to wriggle or wiggle making it easier for me to be absolute and for her to get closer to the nub of him. She asked about tangible things in methodical turn - hair eyes height clothes the way he laughed the way he walked even the way he held his cigarette when he smoked - allowing me to build up a composite that was undeniably so accurate that you could have picked him out in a police line-up or from a queue at a bus stop. None of which mattered to me in the slightest not in terms of Matt or my relationship with him but it was only important to me because I wanted to get it right for Anne to do her justice in a way to ensure I was honest and gave her the fullest picture and even though it was a small thing in itself it became paramount that I was accurate enough to allow her to do what she needed to do with the information to process it in her own way to squirrel it away somewhere I assumed never to be used again even though she closed the conversation by kissing me on the cheek nodding appreciatively and echoing "Well then".

Josh I

"You're happy to talk about it."

I wouldn't say that.

"What I mean is, has enough time passed?"

Will enough time ever pass? I doubt it somehow.

"And yet?"

And yet? Look; it's okay. I've talked about it so much I feel numbed now, anaesthetised. Why should one more interview make any difference? In a way it's like it's not real any more; as if it was just something I imagined.

"I'm sorry."

Yes. Everyone is.

"No. I meant for the questions."

Well… Where do you want to start?

"Salcombe."

Of course.

I wish I'd never entertained the idea. But how was I to know? For Anne and I going down to the coast to camp in Aunt Grace's little Salcombe cottage for the odd weekend here and there was second nature. We'd done it so often since we were children, it was something that went unquestioned. To be fair to old Grace she shared the place around the family; I don't want it to sound like it was our private estate or anything. Most of the time she lived there, you understand, but when she was away - and she travelled a lot - she liked to know it was being looked after. I guess we went there maybe twice a year.

Anyway, one day she rang me to say there was a free weekend in a couple of weeks and asked if I was interested. The timing proved fateful, didn't it? I said yes, partly because I always said yes, but also because there was a girl at work, Claire, I was trying to impress. I thought offering her a weekend away on the coast might just do the trick. I'd broached the subject with Anne when she came to stay the weekend before, primed her to come along to be the potential chaperone just in case Claire needed to know there was a safety net. She had always been a sucker for Salcombe too.

So she agreed and I asked Claire, explaining about Anne. Then Claire said yes too. As it turned out, she probably would have said yes anyway, even without Anne being there. And then Anne called me on the Tuesday before we were due to go, suddenly uncomfortable that she would end up getting in the way, 'playing gooseberry' she called it. I told her it was too late to back out; if Claire showed up and Anne wasn't there the whole thing might backfire with her feeling like it was something I'd planned, a ruse, a trap. Which, in a way, it was. Anne asked me if there wasn't someone else who I could invite, to even up the numbers. Male or female, she said she didn't mind; I think she didn't want to risk being left on her own.

"You thought of Luke?"

Yes, but don't ask me if he was my first choice, I simply can't remember. Concerned that the whole enterprise was about to blow up in my face, I'd have invited Rasputin if it would have done the trick! I mean, it wasn't really Luke's thing. I couldn't see him being comfortable in the cottage, sitting around with us. Anne had met him briefly in the pub the week before, but that hardly seemed a solid enough introduction. Anyway I couldn't have been confident when I mentioned his name. Or even serious. She remembered him. "The quiet one" was how she described him. "Yes," I'd said, "bad taste in shoes." It was a joke he and I had. Anne seemed not totally affronted by the idea. "He was interesting," she said -

though I couldn't tell if by 'interesting' she was using the English or American connotation of the word. We decided to give it a go, so I asked him the next day. He knew Claire - and about what I thought of her. I buttered him up with a line about doing a mate a favour; mentioned that Anne might be there too, so that he wouldn't be alone. He made a show of thinking about it; you know, as if he was really deliberating. And then he said "I've never been to Salcombe" as if that was the clincher. It wasn't, of course.

"But you didn't know?"

Know?

"How he felt about Anne?"

How could I? And how could he? I mean they'd spent - what? - a couple of hours sitting next to each other in a pub; two people in a group of six or seven. They'd hardly exchanged any words from what I could remember, so Luke would hardly have been my choice.

"Your choice?"

As someone Anne might have latched onto. There were more likely candidates. And Luke was hardly her type, given how gregarious she could be. He could come across as a sullen bugger at social events, even though he wasn't really. He just didn't mix well. I used to tell him he had a gene missing or something. But anyway the bottom line was that he said he'd come. Made the 'never been to Salcombe' excuse sounded genuine - though he could have come up with any justification under the sun and I would have believed him; anything that cleared the way for Claire to agree to the trip too.

"So how did it go?"

Depends on your point of view, I suppose.

"Yours?"

If you're talking about me and my 'aspirations' for the weekend - though I know you're not - as well as I could have hoped.

Luke and I went down together. I drove. It was a strange, stuttering journey, long bouts of silence punctuated by bursts of conversation, animation, jokes. Most of the time he seemed preoccupied - though of course it's much easier to make that observation now, isn't it? Then? Well, I'd never done much with him outside of work apart from go to the pub or play the odd game of 5-a-side, so in many respects I didn't know what to expect. Half-way down I was probably having second thoughts - but it was too late then, the die was cast.

We got there late morning. Stopped to get some stuff from a supermarket just outside Torquay. Luke came into his own there, I have to say. Very organised. I would have just thrown things into a trolley, but to my eye it was something he went about with military precision. It was only for a weekend of course, and I knew that there would be loads of Grace's stuff in the kitchen that we could use, but Luke didn't want to leave anything to chance. And I was happy with that. Anything that made the weekend run smoothly and that gave Claire a positive impression was fine with me. We'd offered to give her a lift down too, but she'd arranged to stay with a friend somewhere inland on the Friday night - an old school friend, I think - and said she'd join us just after lunch. Anne said something similar, though her timekeeping could be a bit erratic.

So Luke and I got the place sorted; I showed him where things were; we allocated bedrooms. Although we called it a cottage, it was pretty large. The lounge and kitchen were upstairs and there were four rooms downstairs; three were proper bedrooms, the fourth a study that had a sofa-bed in it. Because I'd arranged it - and because of the hopes I had for the weekend - I took the main room; as the main guest, we agreed Claire should get the second-largest bedroom, and that effectively left Anne with the third and Luke with the study sofa-bed. But he seemed fine with that. Anne and I had probably slept in every room there at some point or another anyway, so it didn't normally make too much difference to us. Once we'd got that all sorted, we walked the short distance into town, just to pass the time. I made an effort to do the guide-thing for Luke, and then we popped into a pub for a pint before we went back to the cottage to wait.

Claire was bang on time. I'd been swinging between hope and despair; one minute convinced the weekend would be great, the next certain it was going to be a disaster. I needn't have worried. As soon as I opened the front door and saw her standing there I had a sense that everything was gong to be alright. Within minutes I knew I could relax and enjoy myself.

"How did you know?"

How does anyone know? A glance? A hand placed on a shoulder? Something said - or not said? Don't get me wrong, we weren't all over each other or anything like that! It was all very subtle, exploratory, as if there was an understanding reached very quickly that said let's just see how this goes, shall we? Do you know what that's like?

"And Luke?"

Luke? He was just Luke. Took charge of making a salad for lunch, made tea, fussed and organised. All the things I was rubbish at - and which I had no desire to be doing right then. It didn't take me long to realise it had been a master-stroke to get him to come along. If I was being selfish - and I was - he gave me the space to focus on Claire. In a good way, I mean.

"And Anne?"

Anne arrived about three-quarters of an hour later. She'd brought some additional provisions too - she always did! - and she and Luke were soon ensconced in the kitchen sorting things out, putting things away, agreeing on a menu for the weekend. They seemed to hit it off okay; almost as if they were old friends I suppose. I was even more grateful at that point because any lingering worries I may have had over how the weekend might be for Anne evaporated.

So we had lunch. It wasn't warm enough to eat outside, but we had the big windows by the dining area open. We could hear the sea and the gulls, the chatter of people as they walked along the path at the bottom of the garden. I guess it was all remarkably easy, civilised, comfortable. I'd had weekends at Grace's where they were anything but that; the kinds of weekends where the first part of Sunday is spent hung-over, and the second part frantically tidying up! This wasn't going to be one of those. I suspect Grace's cottage had never been so well looked after.

Anyway, the girls seemed to get on just fine too. They hadn't met before, but there was enough of a connection to make it work. Claire knew Luke from work and was normally pretty dismissive of him, but I think she cut him some slack. They didn't become buddies or anything like that, but there was enough warmth and tolerance for it to work.

"And Luke, those first couple of hours?"

You'd have to ask him. I didn't really pay him much attention; he was just *there*. As I said, lunch was pleasant; we chatted - though don't ask me about what. Luke contributed here and there, but it was mainly the rest of us I suppose. Sometimes the conversation would be dominated by a pair, as it often is: Anne and I mock-arguing about memories of the place; Anne and Claire talking about 'girl stuff'; Claire and I testing each other out, making discoveries, trying to find out what the rules were.

"You were flirting."

Obviously.

"And after lunch?"

Nothing exceptional. We tidied up and then went for a walk into town. It had got a little bit warmer since the morning so the place was busy; the normal weekend crowds, you know? I don't know about Anne, but when we were there I always felt a little bit superior because we visited frequently, knew the place so well. And we had the cottage. It was almost as if we could say we lived there. It gave us a special status, to me at least. So when we looked in the shops or went into a pub they were the shops and pubs we already knew. We weren't locals obviously, but sometimes it could feel like we were.

For Claire and Luke it was all new, of course. I played the dutiful host with Claire, pointing out things, showing her stuff, describing the place. It gave me an excuse for contact; the touch of her shoulder or arm when I needed to draw her attention to something. It's all part of the game we play, isn't it - exploration of boundaries, the edges of things?

We didn't exactly pair off during that afternoon - I mean, we were together all the time - but we went about the place in pairs, if that makes sense. We stopped for an ice-cream and, when we found a suitable spot, sat by the water watching gulls dive-bombing people who were trying to have their sandwiches in peace.

About four we thought about going back to the cottage. Time had flown by for me, but I'm not sure it had for the others. Anne and I exchanged the occasional glance, both of us trying to check that the other was okay I suppose. She and Luke then explained what we were having for supper - something with prawns if I remember correctly - and then Anne suggested we play games after supper. It was another one of our traditions. Grace's place had a hoard of games from cards to Monopoly and Cluedo. When we used to go there as a family - when Anne and I were younger - we always played games; and it was something we continued to do. Claire seemed keen, Luke probably less so, but we agreed in principle, saying that over dinner we'd settle on the game we'd actually play.

And then, when we stood up to walk back, Claire took my hand.

"Fine, but that's not what I'm interested in."

I'm well aware of that, but I can't tell you what you want to know and extract my story from it. And remember, that whole weekend was driven by me; if I hadn't been there, arranged it, set it up, then - well, then probably nothing. So you can't ignore me and what was important to me.

Everyone wants to know about Luke, but I'm just saying. For the record. Not all the bedrooms were used that night.

And yes, Luke did use the study sofa.

So…

"…"

So we had dinner, which was fine, and then, once we had cleared things away, settled on cards. I hadn't been keen, to be honest; a bit too serious I suppose. But we decided on partner whist which, inevitably, paired Claire and I against Anne and Luke. Anne had always been a bit of a demon with the cards, and I was unsure if Claire was the card-playing sort. I had no idea how we'd fare. In the end, Luke and Anne slaughtered us. Luke seemed pretty solid - I think the game suited his logical style, and he liked rules - and the two of them got into a groove really early. Claire did okay, but it was a good job we weren't playing for money!

At least the wine was flowing, and by the time they'd trounced us everyone was pretty relaxed.

We tried Charades, and then I pushed for a game of something else; loser's prerogative to choose. Something a bit more lively. Anne caught my eye. She knew where I was going with that!

Obtusely, the cottage kept an old version of 'Twister'. I've no idea how it had come to be there nor who had bought it - I mean it wasn't Aunt Grace's kind of game! - but we used to play it loads when we were kids and I always remember it being great fun. Anne made a show of mock protest, but it was Claire's reaction I was most keen on. For obvious reasons…

And before you ask - and not surprisingly perhaps - Luke wasn't keen. The prospect seemed daunting to him. We suggested he be the one who spun the arrow-thing while the rest of us got tied in knots, and he was fine with that. At one point he even produced a camera to take photos of us as we teetered precariously in a really complex tangle awaiting the next instruction that could only cause complete collapse.

Which it did.

As we lay in a giggling heap on the floor, I felt Claire squeeze my hand. It was the signal the evening was over.

"And was it?"

When I eventually emerged in the morning to make coffee for Claire and I, the place was empty. There were signs of breakfast in the kitchen, but Anne and Luke had gone out. There was a note left on the kitchen table. Anne had written down the name of a cafe inland we used to go to occasionally - and a time. I think the note said something like "See you there, or see you here later." She was giving us the option - and ensuring that she was out and about doing something she loved, walking the coast. I had no idea how that would go with Luke. I didn't know if he was a coast-walking sort of person. Indeed, even after the entire weekend was over I'm really not sure I ended up knowing that much more about him. Not until later, anyway.

"And Claire?"

What do you mean, "And Claire"?

"What happened with her? If you want to be sure your 'interest' is recorded, then what happened with her?"

You know very well. Do you just want to hear me say it?

"…"

We split up about six weeks later.

Luke II

And now you are with him again.

When you return, the scene is the same as before. Luke is sitting in the same armchair, adopting the same pose. For a while you had wondered whether or not you would be allowed back, and when you were told 'yes', could not help but try to decipher who had actually made that decision. The last words he had spoken - "well then" - hadn't sounded like those to totally close out a dialogue though there had been a short silence which had quickly metamorphosed into something longer and unbreakable, something that triggered your departure.

Before you take your seat, you scan the desk, the contents of which being the only thing in the room to display any individual identity. You are looking for clues, though clues to what you are unable to say. Everything is neat and tidy as before, though you do get an inkling that the papers (neatly arranged in two piles as before) may have changed their relationship slightly, one being either larger or shorter than previously. But it is only an impression. You cannot be sure. Indeed, there is only one person who can possibly know.

As you sit, you know you now have a reference point; Josh, Anne's brother. And Josh has talked about the weekend to which Luke superficially referred during your first meeting. Doing so had suggested importance back then, and it has become something about which you can triangulate. Validation is critical, the only means you have to uncover the truth. Much has been said in the past, much reported, and there have been conflicting versions of events. Perhaps that is always the way. Stories are like coins, you realise; there are always two sides.

"Tell me about Salcombe."

Salcombe? A popular holiday town in Devon south west England close to the mouth of the Kingsbridge Estuary mostly built on the west side of the estuary an extensive waterfront and sheltered harbour giving rise to its success as a sailing venue and tourism hotspot total population of around three and a half thousand if you ignore the holiday-makers and interlopers. Why?

"You've been to Salcombe."

Statement or question? I've been to lots of places and there are lots of places I could talk about and not just in Devon or England places I've flown to slept in short-haul flights long-haul flights or coach trips there have been coach trips across Europe once or twice but long ago though I still remember the cities and have sepia-tinted memories of Paris or Geneva or Pisa. We could talk about those places too if you would like to.

"Enthralled or in thrall?"

What?

"That's what you said when you were talking about Anne. You were trying to decide which it was."

Was I? Why not both?

"But Salcombe; that's where it started."

Incorrect. It started the moment she walked through the door of the pub. I thought I'd made that perfectly clear. Nothing started in Salcombe. I don't know who you've been talking to though I'm sure it wasn't that Claire woman which narrows down the field somewhat doesn't it but whatever Josh told you couldn't have been true could it?

"Why not?"

Because he doesn't know. Because he can't know. Because although he may have been there he wasn't there as me living my life seeing things from my perspective in the same way as he couldn't have cooked that prawn dish I made whose name I now forget. Because he didn't eat the same ice-cream I ate - I remember it was pistachio I always remember ice-cream flavours - and because he wasn't there on the Sunday morning when we were up and out early choosing to walk the high path overlooking the sea not actually in Salcombe Mr Clever-Dick but elsewhere a short drive away.

"Who drove?"

It was a sunny morning and the house was still quiet. Breakfast was quiet. Coffee and croissants and the radio on low volume classical music just for company really even though we didn't need any company after all why do you need company if you're not alone? And then the question "shall we go for a walk?" as if it was one of those questions that doesn't need an answer because it doesn't because there is only one possible outcome. Have you noticed how many times I've said 'because'? And why is that? It's because - again! - I'm trying to explain things to you because you are asking questions and like a dutiful and friendly and respectful person I am trying to comply to tell you what you want to know even though you are aware of most of the answers and even though I know we've had our differences even if you don't.

" 'Differences' ?"

So it wasn't Salcombe where 'it' started and it wasn't Salcombe where we went for a walk though I will concede that Salcombe was a step along the journey a waypoint where something tangible and intangible happened and which defied words then as it defies words now. Is that better? Is that what you wanted to hear? Though you don't need to answer as I know it isn't enough yet and that there are more questions more prompts and if I don't tell you something else then your questions will continue to come at me so why don't I just keep talking until you tell me to stop or until I see something in your demeanour that tells me I have reached a point where I have said enough and your curiosity is satiated at least for now?

We drove to a place called Hope Something or Something Hope a little way away couldn't have been more than a few miles. We'd left a note telling them we'd be in a coffee shop in Kingsbridge later on and if they wanted they could meet us there at a specified time and then decide what to do next before we had a late lunch and then started to think about heading back because it was a short weekend and everyone had work the next day so there was no real choice in the matter. I doubted they would make it to the cafe but at least we gave them the option and it was a plan which was fine with me because I liked having a plan - and it was especially fine because the plan only involved Anne and I.

And she drove.

We parked in this little place - shall we call it Hope? - and walked away from the village and upwards following the path Anne said would lead to the edge of the land and to where we could see the sea. Why do you go to the coast if not to look at the sea? The first part of the walk the uphill part went through a copse some woods I'm not entirely sure what the correct term should be is it designated based on the number of trees the size of the area or density of undergrowth? How do you know when you're in a forest rather than being in a wood have you even thought of that? And isn't it just a little strange that a wood is named after the thing from which it is made?

She led the way because she knew where we were and going and I followed because that was all I could do given I was lost; lost in the sense of not really knowing where I was geographically and lost in that I was already enthralled in thrall. I walked behind her and watched how she moved I focussed on her feet and her shoes good quality walking shoes that seemed to fit perfectly that showed signs of age of being well used and loved and she seemed sure-footed as she walked up through the trees not speaking at that moment not wanting to trip over a root or something. And I watched her legs the outline of her muscles through the fabric of her jeans the shapes shifting depending on the steps she was taking first a calf then the muscle at the side of the thigh the calf again. And yes I watched her arse too hugged tightly by a seat of denim wonderfully shaped watched it as it moved in front of me close enough to reach out and touch but too far away to do so. Do you know what that feels like? And I wanted to *be* her jeans wanted to wrap myself about her legs to feel the motion of her body to be protecting trapped caressing kissing supporting embracing all those things. Do you know what *that* feels like?

"*Enthralled or in thrall?*"

Shut up. Those are my words. You can't use my words. I forbid you to do so.

"..."

And then suddenly we were out of the woods and onto a plateau of open land where the protection of the trees abandoned us and there was suddenly light and breeze and it was as if we had been released from some kind of prison but my prison was total merciless steadfast and when she paused to allow me to catch up I wanted to run to her to grab her hold her hard and tell her things I didn't have the words for. Or I wanted to run away scared back the way we had come back into the trees and out of the light back into the darkness.

But I did neither of those things. Instead we followed the path to the edge of the land I wouldn't call it a cliff exactly but you might be forgiven for doing so I suppose and we looked out across the sea. We walked and paused and looked occasionally talking about nothing the way you do when there is everything to say when the words you need are impossible to find and so every other word you have ever known is ushered in as inadequate substitutes and I looked at her too quick glances when she was focussed on a ship or a gull wheeling in the sky above us. I looked at her knowing she knew I was doing so. Looked at her hair her wonderful hair the shape of her head the silhouette of her lips against the blue backdrop her cheeks the smallest hint of a dimple when she smiled the elegance of her neck the slope of her shoulders and the hint of her breasts beneath the loose jumper she was wearing.

"…"

You want to know if I touched her. You want to know if as we paused to look out at the sea I reached out to brush her hand her shoulder perhaps to pull her towards me in some rough embrace as if we were movie stars from the fifties or sixties. Do you want to know that or do you wish that was what happened not for me but for you? Is this now your story as much as it is mine? Are you becoming 'invested' in it? Ha, ha!

Well I didn't. We walked and talked walked a little way around the edge of the land which seemed appropriate given I felt as if I was on the edge of something too and at one point I talked about the North Yorkshire coast about how different it was talked about the little villages and towns there places from my childhood and I mentioned their names as if they were somehow magical: Robin Hood's Bay Whitby Saltburn Runswick Staithes. And she said "we should go" just like that as if it was the most natural thing in the world as if the word 'Staithes' had unlocked something had been powerful magical and I felt suddenly as if the world might be a wonderful place after all and that I might have a part to play in it and I said yes we should go. And she said "well then" without breaking stride said it as if a deal had been struck an agreement reached and I was both found and even more hopelessly lost at the same time and I wanted to cry out to shout to laugh all simultaneously but as that was impossible I kept walking and we looped back round back to the path in the woods and this time I went ahead knowing she was behind me her eyes on me as much as the path and I wanted to know what she was thinking but not caring at the same time. Because we had an understanding you see? Even then. And we went back to the car and drove to Kingsbridge and had coffee in the cafe and the others didn't turn up so we went back to the cottage and made lunch and eventually went our separate ways as if nothing had really happened.

"Well then."

Josh II

"You didn't know they were going?"

No-one said a word, so I didn't have a clue. Not that I needed to, of course; I mean, it wasn't as if they needed my permission or anything. But it would have been nice to know.

In a way I'm not surprised that Luke didn't tell me. He kept himself to himself, pretty much. If you'd asked me what he did on his weekends or holidays or when he had some time off, I would have struggled to tell you. I don't think that's particularly odd or unusual with work colleagues, is it? Maybe most people are like that. Oh, they'll tell you when they've done something big - just come back from safari or a trip to New Zealand, stuff like that - the rest of it? On reflection though it just seems a little strange that he was going away for a weekend with my sister and I didn't know about it.

"Would it have bothered you if you did?"

How can I answer that question? Based on what I know now, of course; but at the time? Probably not. I wouldn't have been thinking about him anyway, would I? Anne would have been my primary concern.

"Concern?"

Sorry, wrong word. But you know what I mean.

She was my sister. There are lots of brothers who don't care two hoots what their siblings get up to, but I don't think I'm like that. We're not in each other's pockets obviously - and we weren't really very much alike - but we were close enough back then for one to be concerned about the other.

See, I've said 'concern' again which isn't what I meant. Not really. I would liked to have known, that's all.

"She could have told you."

Yes, she could. And I wondered about that afterwards, once the weekend was over and the news had broken. I guess I was pleased for her then, of course; mildly amused too, given they seemed a bit of an odd couple.

But don't ask me why she didn't tell me what they were planning - or, more accurately as it turns out, what *she* was planning. She just laughed when I challenged her later, so I let it go. It didn't seem important. And, you know what, I don't think it was important, not once they'd been away.

"How was she immediately after the Salcombe weekend?"

I've no idea. We didn't live that near each other, and so when she left the cottage in Salcombe and drove away I didn't see her until much later - 'after the event' as it were. I can't even remember if we spoke on the phone.

No, that's wrong. She did call me a couple of days later to say that she'd had a nice time. Made some positive comments about Claire, just as a sister is supposed to! I know you want to ask me if she said anything about Luke, but I honestly can't recall. And what did I say? Who knows?! I may have made a joke or apologised for her being saddled with him for the weekend, but that would probably have been it.

So there was nothing earth-shattering; no major consequence of those couple of days by the coast. At least nothing obvious. Perhaps in part because I wasn't looking for anything obvious; I was too wrapped-up in my own 'situation'.

"And Anne, did she engineer situations like you?"

She wasn't Machiavellian. Not at all.

I knew about past boyfriends - or those she chose to share with me - and I'd like to think she told me about all of them. Not that there was a large number, you understand. I guess that was one way in which she and I differed. Her relationships were never shallow or experimental, if I can use that word. She wouldn't have done what I did with Claire for example; the 'let's try something out and see what happens' approach just wasn't her style. She operated to a different set of criteria. There had to be depth for her to commit herself; promise or potential, if you like. She once told me that she wasn't about to go into any relationship unless she felt it had the chance to 'be the one'. Being conscious that taking such a step could end up being the last commitment she would ever make to another person was a big thing for her, so she didn't enter relationships lightly.

Ever.

On that basis, her suggesting they go to Staithes could only have meant that something happened that weekend in Salcombe; that there was a connection; that she saw enough in him to take the plunge, to place the bet. And hey, maybe it wasn't a gamble at all. Not at the time. Maybe if I now describe it as a 'gamble' that's just hindsight talking.

Luke III

"Back again?" Is that how you were welcomed when you arrived today? Or perhaps "Back so soon?". Did they say something like that to you, giving you your own personal greeting? As if you were part of the family, almost a fixture.

Or did they say nothing at all?

There's always another question isn't there? Always one more thing to ask. What's that saying about when one door closes...? Perhaps a question is something like a door - especially when you are looking back in time. You get an answer, you find something out, and then just when you think it's done with, it appears nothing is quite that simple.

Luke has been as good as his word, tried to answer your questions, endeavoured to be polite throughout. The gap in knowledge that Salcombe previously represented has been closed, only to be superseded by another: Staithes. Another step on the journey; a gap that can only be filled in by more looking back, by subjecting yourself to the vagaries of hindsight, that unreliable witness.

Rather than immediately join him in the armchairs, this time you walk to the side of the desk and make a show of looking out of the window. It is a ruse, a little game, to see what reaction - if any - you get from him, whether this tactic triggers something different. You have also used the opportunity to take a glance at the papers on the desk, to see if you can discern the nature of any adjustment that has taken place - for again you are certain there has been one. The pages, loose sheets of A4 stare blankly up at you. If anything is written on them - and a shadow beneath their surface suggests this is the case - you cannot make it out as they have been turned face-down.

Playing another card, you ask your question not to him but through the window to the gardens outside, and only when he speaks do you turn and move back to your armchair.

"Did you known what Anne had planned when she contacted you about arrangements for Staithes? I assume she was the one who made contact?"

Why do you make that assumption? Why couldn't I have been the one who made the call? It would have been easy enough to get her number from Josh and call her up ask her about what she said when we were in Salcombe ask her if when she said "we should go" she meant it literally and exactly. I had wondered about that from the moment she walked out of the door on Sunday afternoon about those three words and how much truth they had in them and how much potential too. I don't know if I ever trusted words to be honest or perhaps it was that I'd never thought about them in that way whether or not they were to be trusted until she said what she said and I had to ask myself if she meant it and if she did mean it then in turn what the words themselves actually signified. You could interpret a statement like "we should go" in so many different ways - I know because I tried them all out on the drive back home at work the next day and the day after that manipulated them and their meanings so often as to render them completely useless. And then on the Wednesday it was just after lunch my desk phone rang and it was her saying she had got my extension from Josh and so had been able to get the switchboard to put her straight through and even though I didn't immediately recognise her voice for the first second or two - because telephones can do that to someone's voice - I knew it was her and I knew she was ringing to answer my question.

"Your question?"

About words and whether or not they can be trusted.

"What did she say?"

More words. But words I didn't need to challenge so much - or words that needed to be challenged in a different way. She asked questions mainly. Did I mean what I'd said about Staithes about what it was like how nice it was how it was somewhere from my childhood? Did I mean what I'd said when I'd answered her with "yes, we should go" did I really mean that we should go and that I wasn't just being polite? And did I really want to go to Staithes with her and soon because she had decided she would like that very much and if so then what was I doing the following weekend?

Was it ironic she had as many questions as I did and all of them about the voracity of words too? The words themselves were simple as they often are - a short exchange based on establishing facts and nothing much more.

Except for trust.

"Trust?"

She asked if I would be happy for her to make the arrangements that there would need to be arrangements given it was too far to go for a day trip so there would be things to sort out but if I was happy for her to do so then she would ring me in a couple of days to let me know what the plan was. All I needed to do was to mean what I'd said about "we should go" in a way that in itself actually indicated I meant something more than "we should go" and then on that basis - on that understanding I suppose - she would make the arrangements.

So I said again "yes, we should go" and then "I would like that very much too" hoping that would be enough.

Already I was lost so what else could I do?

"So she called you a second time."

So she called me again. On the Friday just as she said she would. It was a week away our trip but she had the plan and laid it out before me not in all its detail but enough for me to understand to weigh it to be able to react sufficiently for her to judge from my reaction if she was making a good decision because I think there was some of that in her a nervousness something in her voice which told me that this new conversation was another element in her test of me of herself of whether or not she was doing the right thing. And as we spoke her tone changed a little bit - most people wouldn't have noticed - and I felt her relax become more sure as if she was beginning to let herself look forward to something. A voice can do that can tell you things in spite of the words it says or the tone it uses don't you think?

And the arrangements - before you ask - were incomplete but enough to serve their purpose to tell me what was planned and for her to gauge whatever it was she needed to from my reaction. She said she was visiting friends in Durham the day before so I was to get the train to Middlesbrough early on the Saturday morning it meant a change of trains on the way but it was still possible for me to be there by about eleven and that's where she would meet me and then we'd drive to Staithes from there. I had originally wondered about the logistics given we both lived in the Midlands wondered how that would work and had assumed we might travel up together in the car. I had to take a bag with some overnight stuff in it as she'd arranged that we'd stay somewhere overnight in order to make the most of it otherwise it was another long way to go just to look at the sea and eat ice-cream.

"You didn't ask?"

Ask?

"About the overnight arrangements?"

I did not. How could I? That she had a plan and it was all arranged was enough for me.

No. Just seeing her again the prospect of spending time with her the fact that it had been her initiative her choice all of that was enough. She could have turned up with her car packed to the hilt with camping equipment and insisted we sleep on a cliff overlooking the sea being buffeted by wind and rain all night and that would have been just fine too because none of that seemed to matter.

"But there was no camping equipment in the car?"

That sounds more like a statement than a question. Have I told you that before? Has someone else?

It was just a normal car a red car too small to have much in the way of camping equipment in it. When she opened the boot for me to put my bag in there were a few other things in there: another bag more like a large rucksack a coat a scarf an umbrella some walking boots - the same walking boots from Salcombe I recognised immediately. There was room for my bag too and it felt strange throwing it into the back of her car as if in doing so I was crossing a line making a statement or perhaps it was more that she was making a statement by allowing me to do so. An agreement. One completely dissimilar to that concerning where we would stay or the train times or anything practical like that but something bigger more profound more important. Our two bags side-by-side in the back of her little red car felt important though at that precise moment I had no idea of its significance rather it was just a picture an image a set of circumstances of inanimate physical proximity that seemed to mean something.

And then we drove - or rather she drove. It took us about forty minutes to get there. She had programmed Staithes into an app on her phone which sat in its little cradle on her dashboard and told us when we needed to turn right or left or just go straight on. She seemed to listen to it without paying it any attention. There was never any interruption when we were talking she never broke off or diverted her focus away from me in order to concentrate on the electronic voice it was as if she'd known where she was going from the start so we just drove. Do you know how it is when you get in a car to be driven by someone new and it's the first time you've been their passenger the time when you've no idea how good or bad they will be or how fast or slow they might go - or how dangerous. She drove like me that's what I thought. Not fast or slow but appropriately lawfully taking no chances but not afraid to nudge over the speed limit a little bit or a lot when it was safe to do so not that the roads between Middlesbrough and Staithes yielded many opportunities to go fast.

Not far off the main road there's a large car park where you're encouraged to stop and then walk down into the village itself which is a good idea as the roads become steep and narrow quite quickly and if they let everyone drive right down to the harbour it would be carnage because there's nowhere to park and the roads would become clogged in an instant. So we parked and walked down talking a little less at this point because we'd exhausted all the obvious topics on the way - Josh for example - and it felt a little as if the opening gambit was over you know like the beginning in a game of chess where there are some standard moves until someone deviates and then it all becomes unique and unpredictable. Thinking about it now and looking back that's how it felt as if we had finished our opening moves adopted a standard variation and were now waiting for one of us to make the move that would take us away from the book lines.

And as we strolled toward the sea I felt it again that glow she had the same magic that had drawn me to her in the first place. I had been too nervous to feel it in the car I suppose because I was concentrating not on her driving or anything like that but intent on playing my part to be the person I thought she hoped I would be. I tried to remember my lines if you like and not screw anything up not in those first few minutes because that would have been worse than terrible but as we walked down the hill past the little terraced houses the small grocer's the cafes and art galleries I think that apprehension left me as if I'd passed some kind of test perhaps not one of hers but one of my own and in relaxing it was as if my eyes had been opened again. Some of the shops looked interesting but the ones with the most potential were closed for lunch which gave you some idea of the sort of place it was or was then at any rate and so we just paused to look in windows to pick out the places we'd go into on the way back up and then we were suddenly at the harbour and the sea stretched before us and the gulls wheeled in the air reminding me of Salcombe and that wonderful weekend.

…

"You told me about the little art exhibition."

I did?

"So - to use your chess analogy - you made the next move? The explorative squeezing of her hand being your variation from the standard opening."

It didn't feel like that at the time not as if I was doing something calculated because chess is a game all about calculation isn't it? Thinking about it now thinking it about it again as I always seem to be - especially knowing you'll soon return here again asking more questions and wanting more answers - I can't help it and each time I do it seems a little different or I can make it different depending on how I'm feeling or what I want to feel. Isn't that how hindsight works anyway? You kid yourself you're seeing things afresh with new knowledge something that allows you to make sense of your past when really all you are doing is replaying it against a newer set of filters different coloured lenses in your glasses. In a way it isn't that we know more but rather we've a new set of criteria against which to evaluate what happened.

Yes I squeezed her hand but I suspect at the time it was more to say 'thank you' than anything else. Thank you for being there and being there with me thank you for illuminating those fabric scenes and bringing them to life thank you for the Salcombe weekend and the walk we had for the games of charades for the little red car and not having camping equipment in the back of it for the planning and the arrangements and for just being. Now I can make it about anything I want can't I? I can tell you that it was 'a move' part of whatever I had intended part of a devious scheme and if I did would you be any the wiser? Wouldn't you have to believe me because that's what I told you what else would you have to go on other than anecdotes and second-hand testimony from unreliable witnesses? Worse than that would *I* be any the wiser? It's almost a question of which truth you want me replaying for the events you are assimilating and recomposing in your head for a reason I simply don't want to fathom. Why don't you write anything down take notes record the conversations? Where are your pens and papers - because I have mine - and what are you doing with all of my history? What possible use is it to you?

"..."

Did I make the move? The only thing I know is that I squeezed her hand probably for both a million reasons and none. And then she interlocked her fingers with mine. Fact.

"And did it feel like a beginning then, something new? Was it as you'd imagined it to be, or hadn't you imagined it at all?"

Dared to dream? Of course I had dared to dream I wouldn't have been human had I not done so. How do you know if reality is better than a dream because how can you measure a dream ascribe true feelings to it judge it or weigh it? When dreams are good and they turn into reality surely reality can only be better because it's real. I looked down at her fingers linked with mine the structured amalgamation of bone and flesh some of it mine and some not and I squeezed a little again to watch the fingers move to seek the response and to gauge where the sensation came from when she squeezed back. For a moment it was as if my fingers weren't mine at all and I was looking on observing someone else's experiment analysing the results.

When we stepped outside of that little hall we paused on the pavement in my case unsure what was supposed to happen next and then when I looked at her she suddenly moved closer and reached up and kissed me and that kiss became a seal like one of those bright red shiny wax seals that kings and queens would put on the backs of letters in order to designate their authenticity. That kiss - which was slow precise but strangely not passionate - was her wax seal laid upon me and I felt it represented me done and dusted. If in that moment she had sealed my future with her kiss then I was content and all I could do was to hold her my head in her marvellous hair breathing her in to make her part of me and then she broke away laughing her eyes sparkling and dancing in the light and said "let's get lunch!" and led me away from the hall and down toward the sea and a fish-and-chip shop we had previously seen. As as I looked out across the sea again and saw the boats caressing the water it seemed liked a new place a magical place not the village I had known from my childhood at all but somewhere reborn as if I had been picked up and transported to a new world and as we walked to the fish-and-chip shop I understood that I was about to taste the best fish-and-chips I had ever eaten not because they were going to be good but because I was with Anne and she was holding my hand and my future had been sealed by her.

Josh III

"And when you spoke to her next?"

I called her on the Monday. I wanted to know what had happened. Luke had been in work but I didn't have the chance to speak to him. He didn't seek me out, and from a distance - I saw him briefly on the floor where all the conference rooms are - I couldn't tell anything; I mean, there was no wave, no smile. Just like there had been no email, no phone call. Actually it was a pretty manic day as we were closing on a new piece of business, a new contract, and where I worked in pre-sales when we put a bid together or sealed a deal those days were always a little crazy.

So unable to discover anything over the course of the day I rang Anne in the evening.

"What did she say?"

"I thought you'd call". I explained about the day, how I hadn't had time to speak to him. She laughed. "When you do, tell me what he says." I remember that clearly. There was something unusual in her voice; it was a little lighter somehow, not that she was ever monotone or downbeat you understand.

I asked her how the weekend had been, whether or not it had been a success. She laughed again, this time at the use of the word. "Surely," she said, "success depends on what you choose to measure it against." I recall protesting, begging her to be straight with me. And so she took me through the events of the day, sequentially. I could tell she was only focussing on the matter-of-fact, leaving out the nebulous and emotional. There were hints along the way - like how she talked about getting fish-and-chips and then eating them sitting on a bench overlooking the water. It wasn't the words themselves. I couldn't put my finger on it, but I knew something had happened even before she told me. There was the old fashioned in her re-telling of parts of it; "and then he kissed me" she said, as if she had just escaped from a nineteenth century costume drama.

"And are you okay?" I asked her, not really thinking about how she could possibly respond to such a question. Then she laughed again, and I knew she was alright.

"And you?"

Me?

"Were you alright?"

I've no idea to be honest. It was a little difficult to comprehend, Anne and Luke suddenly being an item, and after such a short period of time. I mean they were so different. Luke wasn't her sort of guy, I thought; indeed, I wasn't sure whose sort of guy he might possibly be. But there had been a connection and Anne seemed happy enough.

"And were you - happy enough, I mean?"

Happy? Yes, I guess so. Or probably, no.

I don't know.

I saw Luke the next day - we had lunch in the canteen together - and he was a little bit coy about the whole thing. No, coy's the wrong word. He didn't make a big thing about it, was more factual and dispassionate than I was expecting him to be. At one point he told me how wonderful he thought Anne was, but then he reined himself back in as if he had let something slip. I pushed him for details and got no more than I had from Anne. I asked him "what next?" and he just shrugged his shoulders.

"'What next'?"

I wanted to know what his next move was; what their next steps were. I mean, you can't come back from a weekend away and suddenly be boyfriend and girlfriend and not have any plans.

Did I what?

That was different.

Because Claire wasn't Anne - and I'm not Luke. Our understanding, our approach, our expectations would have been on a completely different scale. It was just a bit of fun really; two people enjoying themselves, each other's company. Don't most relationships start out as something of a lark - or even by mistake - and then turn into something different over time? Often that's all they are, a bit of fun, and so they run their course - usually pretty quickly. But Luke wasn't a 'run their course' person; he didn't do 'larks'. He was probably as serious as anyone I'd ever met. Oh, he could have fun when he wanted to, don't get me wrong. I've seen him as drunk as the best of us - drunker, sometimes - but when it came to something like this, something as important as this, then he was an 'all-in' kind of guy.

"And that bothered you? Because of Anne?"

Anne was an all-in sort of person too. I think that's where she had struggled a bit with men in the past. She'd probably not chosen wisely - if you do 'choose' that is - and those men been a bit more like me; less serious, more temporary. And that never worked out well.

"So surely you should have thought that Luke would have been a good thing for her?"

Looking at it in that way, I suppose so. I just wasn't sure about *him*. I didn't know if he was 'right' for her; if he wasn't too far along some sort of spectrum. I couldn't tell whether or not he'd be able to give her all the things she needed. Oh, seriousness and intensity wouldn't have been a problem as far as Luke was concerned, but everything else?

Perhaps it was balance that concerned me, I don't know.

In any event, she sounded happy. And she could tell I had my reservations, she could hear it in my voice. "Don't worry" she said, "it's all fine."

"And did you worry?"

What do you think?

The Anniversary Party

The question you open with - "Can you tell me about your wedding anniversary party?" - is the only one you need to ask. Even though you did not specify the anniversary in which you are interested, they know all too well, and despite being exhausted from continually reliving an event that happened eleven years previously, John and Margaret ('Mags' to her friends) simply feed off each other the same way a child's clockwork toy, once it has been wound up, marches unstoppably across the carpet until it smacks against the wall. And once there it still endeavours to keep going.

"It was supposed to be such a wonderful day, wasn't it?"

> "It *was* a wonderful day - at least I thought so. We only think of it differently now because of where it's located in time and how it fits in the sequence of things."

"And what happened afterwards."

> "Indeed."

"No, you're right; it *was* a wonderful day."

It feels like a well-rehearsed opening, and you sense at this point there should be a squeeze of hands in recognition of something positive shared; but their hands rest in their laps, too far apart to make such an unseemly gesture. Perhaps it is the constant replaying which - in spite of their words - has taken the gloss from the day.

"It was nice having all the family there, everyone making the effort to come and see us and share our day."

> "June and Catherine worked such wonders with the food, didn't they?"

You wonder if they always start with the food, it's safe territory after all.

"And everyone looked so smart! Your idea of that dress code - bow ties for all the men and bright, flouncy frocks for the women - worked wonderfully well. We looked like a cast of extras from some swish TV drama!"

The look in John's eye suggests that's exactly how he now views it: they were playing parts in a drama, they just didn't know it at the time.

"People were very kind."

"We were spoiled by their generosity, that's true."

"And those crystal glasses Luke and Matthew clubbed together to buy us… Who could have wanted a better present?"

"They make wine taste so much better! Daft isn't it? I'm sure they don't, but it seems that way, to me at least."

"The two of them looked so flamboyant and debonair! I never thought I'd see Luke outshine his brother the way he did that day: that quite remarkable tie he chose to wear was so out of character, and the way he chatted to people… Even Catherine, who had never taken a shine to him, was almost won over."

"Which - being Catherine - was some achievement!"

"I'm not sure that's entirely fair - even if I do know what you mean… But he was so - how would you describe it? - cheerful."

"Cheerful? He was like a different person. As soon as he walked through the door; the way he hugged, shook hands, I could tell something had changed. It was obvious wasn't it? There was something about his demeanour, the tone of his voice."

"You thought he'd won the lottery!"

"I was guessing! There had to be something."

"And it took him an age to tell us."

"He was just making the most of it; stringing us along, knowing we were desperate to find out what had brought about the metamorphosis. Or is that too strong a word?"

"At one point I took Matt to one side and asked him if he knew, but he said he was as much in the dark as we were. The change in Luke hadn't passed him by obviously, but he said he didn't know."

"You sound like you still don't believe him."

"Of course I believed him! How could I not? It was only that I didn't understand how he couldn't know. That's all."

There is a brief silence as if they are trying to recall their lines, to remember where they are in the script.

"You believed Luke when he told you?"

"Yes, of course! It explained everything didn't it? How he was, how he spoke, how friendly he was."

"To everyone, including Catherine."

"Indeed. But love does that, doesn't it? It did for me, don't you remember?"

"How could I not?"

John's hand moves and makes the long journey across the sofa to where Margaret is sitting. It is a gesture which allows them to regather their thoughts. He looks at his wife as if certain he knows what they are supposed to say next.

"But I still don't understand - even after all this time - why he didn't bring her. She was a lovely girl and would have been perfectly at home at the party, fitted right in, made the day even more special."

"You know why. He explained. And then Matt endorsed that explanation after they'd had their chat, once he'd found out. Luke's reasoning - his excuse, if you like - was consistent."

"That their relationship was still new? That he hadn't quite 'worked her out yet' - whatever that was supposed to mean! Did you buy that? Do you accept it even now?"

"Why not? He may have been on cloud-nine, but that didn't stop him being Luke underneath: cautious, rational, averse to risk-taking. If Anne was the biggest thing that had ever happened in his life, why wouldn't he want to be protective of it? Of her?"

"But we're not ogres."

"I'm not saying we are; and to be fair, Luke never said we were either. We met her soon enough anyway, didn't we? We had that really nice weekend when they came over to stay. When was that, about a month later?"

"It would have been nice if Matt and Stella had been there too. It would have been the one chance we would have had to be together, all six of us."

"But it was hard for them wasn't it, Luke and Anne living and working apart for such a long time? And then not being close to Matt and Stella. Coordinating a gathering with so many variables isn't easy.

There is something in the tone which suggests someone who knows they are not on solid ground, quicksand from which they have needed to be rescued on more than one occasion. The marching clockwork toy has just about reached the wall.

"Other people manage it; at Christmas or Easter. Yes, we saw them as couples, which was nice, but never all together. And before you say anything, I know there were excuses about University finals, and then finding jobs, moving home - for each of them except

Luke, of course - and I know all those things take time and are disruptive. I know that. But they could have tried a little harder couldn't they? And then before you know it, months have turned to years. Christmases pass - how many? Three? Four?"

"Before what?"

"Before it was too late?"

"Come on; you talk as if it was our fault somehow. Never mind us, it was even quite a while before the four of them managed to meet, remember?"

"Remember? Ambleside! How can I forget? Even though we weren't there, even though that was nothing to do with us…"

Ambleside. A new word, delivered as if it is code for something meaningful. You note it down, mentally; it is something to clarify. For a moment you feel like a detective who has just been handed a clue.

"You know, I do think it was our fault in a way. We should have insisted, told them all to come and see us - together. We had a right to do so, but we didn't. We might have been able to help. After all this time, that's the one thing which still torments me; the thought that we might have been able to make a difference."

And then they fall silent, the clockwork motor finally run down.

Luke IV

You had deliberately left him with your request, left it like a parting shot as you stood at the door about to turn the handle.

"I want to hear about that first night together" you had said, "but not now. The next time I come." And having twisted the knife somewhat, you left expecting him to bleed, to suffer as he replayed that evening as he surely had many times before.

Wasn't that a little cruel, to make him stew like that? Perhaps; but you want to be certain you get as close to the truth as possible, and you believe the more he engages with his own story, the more he will remember, the closer he will get you to something authentic, original. You are concerned that any sudden response, made off-the-cuff without sufficient time for reflection, will not necessarily be accurate, and you hope that in this case the application of hindsight - layers and layers of it probably! - will varnish and polish the truth.

It shouldn't be shabby or tawdry; not this part.

Where should I start? I have been asking myself that question. What should I do with all the time between us sitting eating lunch always a wary eye on the gulls and later after the drive and the dinner. It would be easy to skip straight through to the climax as it were but that would be to ignore the context the foreplay if I may be so bold context offered by the passing of time or the ticking down of the clock context which needs to be understood if you are to have any chance of seeing things from my perspective.

So we ate fish-and-chips then scrunched up the few remaining chips in the paper found the nearest rubbish bin then walked along the edge of the sea the slipway past the pub to the steps up to the cob and then out along it because that was the thing you were supposed to do. And all the while we were holding hands and talking pointing things out and though the language we were using was mundane enough indeed almost more mundane than it needed to be it became a sort of code as if all the real words were hiding in plain sight in the subtext underneath. In a way we were asking questions without asking them discussing the colours of the small boats at anchor bobbing on the water wondering how the birds' nests were wedged into the cliff face all comments on other things as if we were filling in a paint-by-numbers in a supremely abstract way.

I want to say that at one point there was a comment about "The French Lieutenant's Woman" as that would have been entirely appropriate given elements of its story line even if we were hundreds of miles away from Lyme Regis. I want to say that but I'm not sure if I can because I do not know if that is a misremembering or a real remembering or some totally fictional notion brought about because we were walking on a cob and how it seems the kind of thing we should have been saying. Hindsight is no aid when you're not even sure if there is a 'thing' to be remembered and therefore knowing if recall needs to be sharper or more factually correct is an impossibility.

What is undeniably true is that time passed as we strolled and once or twice we paused to kiss again as if to restate that we were there that we were together that we had reached an accord an agreement an understanding. And as time passed and I watched others walk the cob watched the boats on the sea the birds flying into and out of their secret nests in the cliff-face I knew the hour was approaching slowly or quickly (I can't recall which) when one single question growing in importance for me would inevitably be answered. It was a question that just a few hours previously had been so totally unimportant that it hardly earned a mention - did I mention it? - one which centred on Anne's arrangements for the evening because discovering what she had planned not only resolved an increasingly pressing and material uncertainty about how we would navigate from Saturday to Sunday but also shed light on how she had approached the day and her expectations for it. No. More than that. Her ambitions for it.

But I'm jumping ahead a little.

We walked back up the hill taking our time going into two or three of the little shops and galleries that were now open. It was one of those expeditions where you go into a place demonstrating all the outward signs that you might be buying something indeed telling yourself that you actually *want* to buy something but knowing deep-down that you will not. So we pointed at paintings flicked through prints thirty or forty deep in those free-standing display racks galleries have picked up little sculptures of ducks marvelled at glass paper weights at one point Anne even entered into conversation with a shop owner expressing an interest in the background of one particular artist trying to gauge how old they were their history as if doing so might influence whether or not she bought something.

Eventually we regained the car park finding the car exactly where we had left it nothing in our hands except each other's. "It's not far" she said as she turned on the engine and I remember looking at my watch to see what the time was not that it made any difference other than to tell me how much of it we had to navigate between then and the next way-points on our journey. As we pulled out onto the main road I tried to list them in my head: arriving at wherever it was we were staying then having dinner then the rest of the evening nighttime sleeping and in the morning what then? My vision fell off a cliff at that point though to be honest it was hardly crystal clear between now and then anyway the only truly real thing to me at that moment was the certainty that I was sitting in a car being propelled forward driven by Anne who had programmed something into her sat nav and who therefore was in her own way in the hands of someone or something else.

We followed the road south and occasionally saw the sea and signs that said Whitby and Scarborough more places from a slice of my childhood each with their own histories and myths though it was only Whitby I really remembered because of the Goths the jet the abbey and the stories of Dracula my father used to tease me with. We swung off the main road a couple of miles outside of the town and followed a narrower one for a short while before pulling into the car park of what looked like a cross between a pub and a hotel though if you'd pressed me to choose I would have said the former. Anne caught me looking at my watch again and asked if I had somewhere I was planning to get to and then she laughed and got out of the car walking round the back to get the bags out. It was already nearly six and I realised that the time had been passing quickly and we had sauntered and strolled and not rushed when looking in the shops and I knew it was time well spent and then considered for a moment that notion - the spending of time - as if it was a currency. And perhaps it was and if so then the obvious question which had to follow was how much more of my outstanding balance would I be spending with Anne because at that precise moment I think I would have willingly given it all to her.

I took the bags then she locked up the car and I followed her toward the building and in through a glass-panelled door that had a small sign above it that said 'Reception'. There was a hallway with a desk in it and further on I could see the bar proper and some tables disappearing off to the left which were laid out for diners. As I was looking busying myself feigning interest in some prints of the sea that were hanging on the wall opposite the desk each one adorned with a small label and a price tag a woman appeared and spoke to Anne the result of the conversation being the handing-over of keys the sound of which made me turn to see them beginning to walk toward a set of stairs off to the side Anne looking back at me her smile demanding I follow them. At the top of the stairs there was a small corridor and the woman led the way to its end where she unlocked another door. The room was spacious with windows on either side which made it very light and there was a large bed a small desk-cum-table with a chair and lamp and against another wall a large settee which was clearly convertible into a sofa bed. At one end of it pillows and bedding had been neatly arranged. As I put the bags down the woman showed Anne the en-suite bathroom and exchanged information about times for breakfast and asked if we would be dining. She glanced at me before saying 'yes' and suggested that perhaps a table about seven would be appropriate and all I could do was nod in agreement at which point the woman left as if I had delivered a cue.

"Well then," she said walking back to where I had left her bag on the bed unzipped it then pulled out her clothes her wash-bag. Without saying anything else she opened the top drawer in a set of drawers that were opposite the bed and began putting her things in leaving out those items that needed to go into the bathroom and those she wanted to place on the bedside cabinet: a book a small alarm clock. Following her lead as it seemed I had for the entire day I mimicked her actions though obviously taking the second drawer down and the bedside cabinet nearest me on the right-hand side of the bed. It was a strange experience this unpacking and putting away not in the act itself but that I was doing it at all that we were doing it together in concert for the first time and I couldn't help but wonder whether this might prove to be the only time such an event occurred and so I tried to savour it to take in every nuance and movement to analyse define absorb the distances between us as we moved about how they fluctuated and whether or not the space we did not occupy was charged feeding off something intangible and nameless. It was activity that was over in a heartbeat and then she suggested we go and have a drink before dinner immediately filling any awkward gap before it had a chance to appear. As I reached her side she stopped me and kissed me and although brief it was a different kiss not the sort of kiss that one would share on the cob at Staithes but something more private one that in itself represented a step a progression a further signature on our invisible agreement as if we were moving from having our names written in pencil towards signing them in ink but being half-way along that journey I had no idea what medium we might be using. Checking she had the key to the room she waited for me to open the door and as we left we both glanced to the settee and the folded linen and she laughed and I felt a little closer to answering the question I had surfaced about her ambition.

Don't ask me what we had to drink because I can't remember. I don't normally suffer from nerves not in the sense of stage-fright nerves nor those that relate to the moments before a big exam. I was never discomforted in that way as a child and I suppose I was able to carry that equilibrium through into adult life so even before interviews for jobs I seemed able to maintain a balance to remove myself from the relative importance of what was going on and the implications of the outcome whichever way it went. It was a distancing I suppose a mechanism for detachment that allowed me not to get too passionate about things and by being dispassionate I always found myself able to focus on the task in-hand the important question and the even more important answer. Call it a skill or a technique if you want to but that was the way I was made I suppose not that it ran in the family as far as I could see. Matt was never able to stand back like me.

But that evening was different especially as we sat there drinking whatever it was we drank making small-talk and waiting for the clock to tick round closer to seven so that we could go and have dinner the crossing of another threshold another step closer to finding the answer. Oddly I do remember what I ate or what we ate because independently we chose the same things as if that might be taken for a sign: scollops to start and then crab ravioli. Did I take it for a sign? Perhaps I did perhaps I thought it was prescient demonstrated something about two people actually meant to be together wasn't it supposed to work like that when people are in synch not symbiosis or anything as fanciful or esoteric as that but an indication of alignment. Maybe that was why as we sat and ate dinner I began to relax a little more could feel myself doing so even though the time was ticking on and soon enough we would abandon the table and make our way back upstairs to our room the room Anne had booked the room with the extra bed which allowed her to cover all bases keep her options open and mine too I suppose if her planning actually went that far. Or maybe it was the beer or whatever I'd had before the meal that relaxed me alcohol on an empty-ish stomach combined with the couple of glasses of white wine we'd had during the meal not that there was any sense of needing Dutch courage just in case you might be jumping to that conclusion. Even in hindsight I can't see those glasses of wine in that light.

It was still relatively early when we finished diner. We decided not to have another drink and so there was very little left to do. It wasn't exactly light but we still went outside and walked down the road a little way towards the sea not really talking very much just using the walk as an excuse to pass some time not to put anything off exactly but to avoid the awkwardness of "what do we do now?" when we got back upstairs. So we walked and held hands and then after a while I had to stop and pull Anne to me and we kissed in the half-light on a deserted road kissed in a different way a harder way our tongues perhaps for the first time really trying to find answers delving discovering as if they had minds of their own as if they were explorers sent out to find something - the source of the Nile perhaps! - and report back. And they did or mine did and after a few moments we stood there just holding each other breathing quietly then Anne pulled herself away released herself and began to walk back towards the pub her hands now swinging gently by her side me following along about three paces behind her.

I remember she said "do you want to go first?" when we got back to the room. The door had closed behind us and we had kissed again a different softer kiss to the one we had just shared on the lane outside and she had kicked off her shoes and indicated the bathroom and said "do you want to go first?" in a way that meant I was going first whether I liked it or not. I'm sure I must have smiled as I picked up my wash-bag and walked into the en-suite. When I closed the door and looked about it was as if I had never been in a bathroom in my life a strange sensation almost as if I had no idea what I was supposed to do nor what "going first" actually meant. The face that stared back at me from the mirror seemed as lost as I was in spite of the smile hidden just beyond the lips the glint in the eye and so I tried to shake myself into action and went to the toilet filled the sink with hot water washed my face my hands emptied the sink and then brushed my teeth. I asked myself if that was enough if there shouldn't be something else I ought to be doing and even though I didn't think so I applied a little body spray to my chest not because I felt smelly nor because I had any great urge to stink like a polecat but because I thought it might be nice for Anne. There was a fraction of a second when I realised I didn't actually know if that was nice or not whether I should have done that or not and I could have panicked perhaps I did panic for a fraction of a second but then I found myself opening the door and tried walking back into the room looking confident or comfortable something like like. Anne was sitting on the edge of the bed reading her book her own wash-bag at her side the fabric of some garment or other resting in her lap and when she didn't immediately look up on my reappearance I knew that my effort to seem comfortable and in control had been somehow wasted. When she finished the sentence or paragraph she was reading and finally looked at me she smiled and said "my turn" as if she was about to go through the same process the same uncertainty the same dilemma as I just had.

In terms of nightwear I had brought loose boxers pyjama bottoms a baggy t-shirt uncertain of what I would need where we would be staying knowing I had to be flexible. There was even an old sweatshirt just in case my image of Anne's car being filled with camping equipment had proven uncannily accurate. I changed into the t-shirt and pyjama bottoms because they seemed the most appropriate I had no desire to appear too sure of myself I wanted to feel natural somehow and I didn't have the sort of body I could impress someone with. As I threw the boxers back in the drawer I caught a glimpse of the settee and the sofa bed and realised they were as they had always been and it occurred to me the reason Anne might have sent me into the bathroom first was because she had wanted time to unfold the sofa and turn it into a bed so that it would be plain to me when I emerged where I was sleeping what the deal was and that we hadn't actually concluded anything. But she hadn't done so and the settee was still just that and so I sat on the edge of the bed and stared at it at the sheets and unneeded pillows and in that moment felt as if the answers to all those questions I had been posing since the beginning of the day were now visible in a set of bedding that had not been unfolded.

The sound of the ensuite door opening stole my attention away from the sofa and the contemplation of what might have been from an alternative version of reality to the one where Anne now stood framed in the doorway wearing a nightshirt buttoned up the front granddad collar the bottom of it ending about half-way down her thighs revealing legs that surprised me with their shape their length their nakedness. She was carrying nothing. I stood not out of choice but instinctively as if compelled to do so as if standing was the only possible option and I tried to take her in all at once only to find it impossible to do so my eyes not being able to absorb the totality of her in one go. She paused smiling knowing the effect she was having on me certain as to how I would react and I sensed that the rest of the evening was already mapped out if not specifically part of her plan then the undeniable consequence of it.

I walked over stopped perhaps a foot in front of her and she said "hello" not as if we had just met for the first time but rather as if she were making a different introduction one that signalled not the passage of time but rather a transition between things. She put a hand on my arm and I copied her not to mimic but in response as if her action had given me permission to do so and having made that first move that initial contact then everything else became suddenly permissible. I ran my other hand through her hair my fingers tracing down to her neck felt the shape of her shoulders through the pastel blue material and as if my fingers had a will of their own down to her chest to feel the rise of her left breast its nipple beneath the soft fabric. She pulled me closer we kissed at first softly considerately and then gradually the kiss became deeper more intense hands moving to our backs to confirm the embrace to define shoulder blades the gradual tapering of bodies down towards the waist and though her hands stopped there mine continued to the hem of her nightdress and then beneath it finding the flesh at the back of her thighs and then upwards to the curve of her buttocks and the edge of her knickers. And as I squeezed gently she broke away from the kiss and took hold of my t-shirt and pulled it upwards forcing me to break my hold as I raised my arms to allow her to pull it off me. Once freed my hands found the top button on her shirt and gently loosed it and then the next the next each one a promise revealing a little more of her cleavage until they were all undone and I could ease the material away back over her shoulders revealing her perfect breasts their darker nipples hardened rough to the touch first of my fingers and then my lips as I bent forward to kiss them to envelop them to dance around them with my tongue and all the while her hands in my hair on my shoulders encouraging steering then one of them down to the top of my pyjamas exploring through the cotton the extent of my erection now fierce and undeniable. I traced the edge of her panties and then moving to their centre found the flimsy material already moist my fingers rubbing gently trying to find a rhythm and as I did so she eased my bottoms down over the ridge of my waist so that they fell to the floor and as I stepped out of them so she slipped from her knickers and then led me to the bed where she lay down and pulled me toward her. From that moment we were both lost frantic compelled on a collision course of sorts impossible to show restraint as if we were being chased by time itself and so we kissed and clung and kissed exploring flesh and more flesh her fingers at one moment near my groin my penis mine around her breasts and then down between her legs into her moist vagina as if they were searching for a secret. And then suddenly arriving near to the point of no return I found myself hovering over her and she sensed my hesitation and whispered "it's okay" and then guided me inside her beginning to arch as I began to push myself further into her then up on my arms looking down pushing and thrusting her legs now bent feet round my sides urging me on her eyes closed her mouth open her hands now above her head clinging to the headboard her moaning louder as I pushed further and further as if there was a place I had to get to always out of reach and then suddenly in a rush the explosion mine push push and push again emptying myself into her as if I wanted there to be nothing left of me as if I wanted her to have all of me and then one last moan from her from me and I fell forward collapsed my head beside hers my chest against her breasts my hips kissing hers and I knew then what it was like to be alive that I would never have another such moment that I had discovered something I could never afford to let go.

Equilibrium

If you are honest with yourself, the boundaries of your meetings with Luke are beginning to blur, as if they are becoming one long session. And although he is at the heart of the maelstrom, you are using others' testimony to give context to his narrative: Josh, Luke and Matt's parents - and soon Stella and perhaps others, who knows? They are like punctuation marks designed to stop a text from running away with itself and getting out of control.

That they suggest sequence is a deceptive fallacy. In some ways they represent structure, one the consequence of another rather than the parallel experience which in many ways is what they should be. In order to get a true picture of what happened that weekend in Salcombe shouldn't you have listened to all the voices simultaneously rather than in a manufactured sequence? After all, it's bad enough that their statements are flawed, interlaced with hindsight and misremembering. If there was a court to judge them, perhaps they would fail to stand up to scrutiny. Or are you that court? Judge and jury?

What happened after Staithes? Isn't that the next question? And the answer is, inevitably, nothing and everything. Nothing, in that life went on; everything, because it all led somewhere. Every last morsel of it led here.

"What happened after Staithes?"

Luke: Nothing and everything.

Josh: Anne called me the next day, after I'd seen Luke at work. I'd asked him how the weekend had been and he seemed a little vague, so I tried to get hold of Anne and she rang me back that evening. I hadn't been worried, not really, but I didn't like not getting the whole story - or not enough to put my mind at rest, to understand what was going on. When I found out - once I put together the various clues they had supplied me with - I confess to have been a little surprised; like I said before, they didn't seem a natural couple. Chalk and cheese. But Anne appeared generally buoyed by the whole thing, upbeat, and so there was nothing for me to do was there? I tried to see Luke in a new light, to cut him some slack, to see if I could uncover something attractive in him that I'd missed - because Anne certainly had. She was cautious, careful, not reckless like me. She liked to know that the odds were stacked in her favour before she placed a bet. Me? Too often I'd just let the whole lot ride and see where I ended up. If we *had* been gamblers, then only one of us would have made any money. Or at least that's what I used to think. And for a while after too.

Stella: I only found out later, of course, not that Staithes had anything to do with me; not then anyway. I must have picked up the news of Luke's conquest from Matt a little while after. I'm pretty sure that was the word he used, 'conquest'. He'd said it as if it were a joke, as if it was the last thing Anne could possibly have been. There was no way his older brother was capable of anything as normal as that, not in Matt's eyes. I remember him speculating about what sort of a girl Anne must have been, notions he was able to embellish or disprove when he quizzed Luke a couple of weeks later at their parents' wedding anniversary. I think he had been expecting to meet her there - well, we both had - but she hadn't shown. That seemed a little strange I suppose; I mean why wouldn't Luke want to show her off? In the end Matt was forced to grill his brother in private in order to garner as much information as he could. He wasn't given much of a picture - at least that's what he told me - but the official line the family adopted was that Luke seemed in a better place and that was all that mattered. It was something of a 'kid glove' stance on reflection, and obviously knowing what I know now I can see why. I'm pretty sure Matt made some comment about her having to be a benevolent witch to cast such a spell on Luke. It was a joke, of course, but maybe it sewed a seed. Then everyone let it go; it became normal pretty quickly, just as these things do. People stopped talking about Luke and started talking about Luke-and-Anne even if she remained invisible, something of a mystery for a while.

John & Margaret: We had a party and Luke came on his own. But we've told you that already, haven't we?

Luke: Staithes didn't finish with that first explosion the explosion that was as much mental as it was physical. You ask the question as if you want to rush on to brush the rest of the weekend under the carpet as if everything that happened in the twenty-four hours or so after about nine-thirty on the Saturday evening was an irrelevance. I don't think that does any justice to the weekend its events or to Anne and me come to that. It doesn't recognise in any way how momentous those few hours were nor how the passage of time even a relatively short amount of time less than two days can turn your world upside down and not only that but change the course of your life as if someone had thrown a lever for a set of points on the track on which your train was travelling and suddenly you're off in a new direction heading somewhere else. Isn't that what they say life's about those special moments the changes of direction the opportunities the opening up of new vistas so that you find yourself exploring new things you hadn't expected to encounter? Well initially that's what it felt like the whole day up to that crescendo - which was the real throwing of the switch - and then the commencement of the journey that followed a journey that when you're on it you never imagine might actually be a siding that could possibly end with a set of buffers because we like to believe or maybe we're conditioned to believe our journey is a continual one never-ending with those moments those opportunities spaced out in front of us where our lives could go left or right. Perhaps I'd always expected my life to be a constant leaning to the left and then along came Anne and she took me in another direction altogether.

When we made love again more slowly more considerately it felt like another first time as if the previous first time had belonged to someone else motivated by something else we'd needed to get out of the way in order to begin properly which is what I'd like to think we then did. Taking our time we explored without any hurry almost as if we had nowhere at all to get to. It was a celebration of ourselves of each other and the real magic of it was in deciphering the bodies we were inhabiting the vehicles that led to so much else. I got to begin to understand the real shape of her breasts the way they curved their relationship to her shoulders and the rest of her the shape of her hips and the symmetry of the pattern they made between torso and legs tracing the extent of her as you would a graph on a sheet of paper if you were attempting to understand the formulae that made the line. And it was a lot like that - I see that now - an attempt to deconstruct what made her a challenge an endeavour that I was certain would take me the rest of my life and still I would get no nearer to the essence of her. Yes I would understand more of her on the surface a surface I could revel in bury myself in her smell her touch uncovering her secrets like the crown of her hair the folds of her vagina the way the second toe on each of her feet overlapped her big toe a little more than perhaps was normal. But all of these things were just superficial and although they were what aroused me made me excited fuelled my desire for her a part of me knew they were ultimately nothing and that the real prize was to be had elsewhere if only I could learn to translate it. Did she feel the same about me? I don't know but I doubted it given I'd always seen myself as a shallow individual and that what she saw was what she got and that there was little of any real substance beyond my physical presence but if that proved to be enough at least as a starting point supplemented by even the most modest of additional if invisible attributes then that was fine. I could work on the rest.

So we made love again and then laughed and snuggled and whispered and eventually fell asleep and in the morning as if surprised to find our selves there on the east coast in a hotel bed together we fell into a semi-hasty encore needing reassurance perhaps before we went down to breakfast after a shower holding hands feeling a little guilty assuming that it was blatantly obvious to the young girl who served us orange juice coffee and toast what we had been up to. Later walking through Whitby on our journey south and back to the workaday world that had suddenly ceased to be real and meaningful we went through the motions of looking at boats on the water (again!) the jewellers selling jet the Goths loitering outside fish-and-chip shops and I for one wondered what any of this had to do with us because we had moved beyond that we had transcended the mundane. On this new spur line - sent there by the throwing of those points remember! - there were different things to explore a new world to conquer new rules to write and old rules to be torn up and thrown away. For me everything began afresh with Anne. I began afresh because of her reborn almost like learning to walk again or talk again or like looking in a mirror and having to come to terms with the face that faced me which was in its way another new relationship.

"So there was a new equilibrium?"

Luke: 'Equilibrium'? Are you even listening?!

Josh: I suppose you could say that, though equilibrium's always been over-rated in my opinion. Where's the fun in that? Was Anne a different person; is that your question? I suppose so. I saw a little more of her of course; after all she had a reason to come to town now, not that she stayed with me any more. It was probably two or three weeks after their Staithes weekend that I saw her next, and they were definitely 'an item', she and Luke. It was proof enough, how they behaved together, as if proof were needed. He seemed little changed on the surface and it was only when she was around him that you could see anything resembling a transformation - and even then it was a modest one. But there were evenings of laughter and camaraderie, and on balance I have to admit that I was pleased for her.

There was no talk of plans, not for a long while, though there shouldn't have been any surprise in the fact they took their time; Anne jokingly called it "wearing each other in". It was their modus operandi, both of them. Cautious, considerate, not wanting to make any move that would be unduly risky or precipitous. Months passed before I had the first inkling that one of them might move so that they could live together. I had assumed it would be Luke, to be honest. He was so in thrall that she could have asked him to do anything - or at least that was my impression. And there was nothing special about his job, where we worked; I didn't feel he would be missing anything by just getting up and walking away. When I challenged her later, Anne said she had been in a similar position, though I'm not sure I entirely bought that. She said she wanted a change, was bored with what she was doing, so why shouldn't she be the one to move? She also enjoyed the major advantage that the firm she worked for had offices where we lived and so it was just a matter of asking for a transfer. It sounded easier than I suspect it actually was, but the logic was faultless. I always wondered if Luke put his foot down; if he did, then that was rare enough. Maybe the tie-breaker was that he liked change less than she did.

Stella: Equilibrium? I guess you could say that, though I'm not the person to ask, am I, given I didn't really know them at the time nor what they were moving from and to. And, to be frank, I didn't really care. Matt seemed disinterested too. There had been a short period where he had been intrigued more than anything else, but when events conspired to keep us apart - as a foursome, I mean - well… It wasn't as if he was suffering or losing out personally because his brother suddenly had himself a serious girlfriend. There was no history under threat.

Luke: Sorry for the outburst but you ask the question - 'equilibrium' - as if it were simply a matter of flicking a switch turning something on or off and there you have it voila bingo all sorted. When there's an earthquake a big one and buildings crumble and roads crack great holes appear and people fall inside them cars too and maybe what's left of the buildings that have already fallen down. Would you say that was a new equilibrium? There's shock and panic and people trying to understand what's going on and then after that there's the coming to terms the deciding what to do how do we bury the dead repair the roads rebuild the buildings and it's not until you've done all of that you get to a new normal everything between the before and after is something else limbo purgatory it's where you find your way. Not that what happened in Staithes was negative in the way an earthquake is in fact quite the opposite but it hit me like one and in hindsight maybe I did wander around metaphorically trying to regain my bearings to see what of my old life Anne had raised to the ground and therefore what I needed to rebuild or salvage - or what I recognised I now needed to build for the first time.

Did all this lead to a new equilibrium, as you call it? Yes but it came gradually from the rubble of my old life it took time and even when I may have felt I had reached that position that new balance - not that I'm sure I ever did by the way not consciously at least - then perhaps even then it was still unstable. I know I can say that now not just because of what happened later but because of the sort of person Anne was one constantly challenging inventing surprising me forcing me to look at things differently all the way from that fabric landscape in Staithes' little art show to just about everything else. Everything else. My entire frame of reference had been disassembled before my eyes shattered blasted to smithereens exposed for what it was an existence that had been inadequate based on premises and prejudices I didn't understand and assumptions I didn't know I had made. Can you comprehend what that feels like to be stripped bare of the tenets by which you have lived your life to be shown afresh what really matters what life is all about what it could be all about to have your value-system adjusted turbo-charged in some ways to find yourself walking around looking at everything through new eyes like clouds and grass and shop fronts the headlights on cars the way the spines of half-read books were bent the shape chewing gum made when it had been trodden into the pavement? That's why I say it was gradual that it took time that I felt like I had been reborn reinvented that there was a new me hatching from inside the shell of the old one. I think it's going on even now even after all this time and all the things that have happened. Can you understand that? For all your questions and the theories that must lie behind them for all your cleverness your detachment even your superiority I'm not so sure you can.

John & Margaret: Equilibrium? It seemed that way, I suppose, at least based on what we'd heard. The news filtered through, mainly second-hand from Matt, occasionally from Luke himself.

> In the beginning there was a fair amount of opinion from Matt if I'm honest these seemed laced with incredulity. I don't think he'd ever given his brother the credit he deserved.

For what?

> But it didn't take long for Matt to lose interest - just a couple of weeks. Less probably. He was always the more self-absorbed of the two. After that we were largely relying on the odd phone call from Luke.

We badgered him to bring Anne to visit, to let us set-up a family gathering. You know she didn't come to our anniversary party?

> We've said that already.

But we got the impression that there'd been a shift, yes, and for the better too. I don't know if that's what you mean by equilibrium, but that's how you could choose to interpret it.

> And when we finally met Anne

- some considerable time later, it must be said -

Indeed. When we finally met her we could instantly see why she'd made such an impact, and why Luke was completely besotted with her. She was unlike any of his previous girlfriends.

Not that there had been that many. Or not that we knew about, or had met. He'd always been something of a closed book. Often they were no more than names; at times we even wondered if they were real!

He wasn't a fantasist or anything like that, you understand. I don't think he invented people.

So to actually meet Anne - and more than once too - well, that said something didn't it?

You make him sound - I don't know - unsavoury.

'Unsavoury'?

Shady; not trustworthy. Almost deceitful. And, as I just said, I don't think Luke was ever deceitful, not in the sense of being deliberately dishonest. He played everything with such a straight bat. Do you know what I mean?

Not that Matt was dishonest either.

That's not what I'm saying. Perhaps you might choose to think of Luke as a believer in things, and that when he believed in something - I mean, *really* believed in something - then he was unshakeable, almost obsessive. He would brook no challenge, no questioning.

And that's exactly how he was with Anne - not that we needed to challenge or question, you understand. In his eyes she was beyond reproach, beyond question, beyond doubt.

And we could understand that a little, his point of view I mean.

Luke: I don't know who you mean by 'people' after all this wasn't about 'people' it was only ever about me and Anne - or at least that's how it was for the next few months. No-one else needed to do anything it was our thing my thing. Others were proprietorial wanted a piece of the action a slice of the pie they wanted a part of Anne at least that's how it felt but at first I wasn't ready to share how could I be if I still hadn't really worked out what I'd landed or got myself into? I was still trying to sort things through to work out how we worked how we could or would work and yes some of that was about mundane things like where we lived and when we saw each other and where we went for holidays or weekends away the films we saw all of those sorts of things but everyone has to go through that when they 'adjust' (to use your word!) to a new 'equilibrium' (your other word!). Matt pestered for a short while but it was easy to fend him off as I knew he'd lose interest but I had to keep feeding Mum and Dad snippets trinkets making promises about next month or the month after that until I was ready until I understood. You might ask whether that was just me being insecure the kind of question that's easy to ask in hindsight when you've got nothing to lose - from your side I mean not mine. And you might be right maybe I was insecure perhaps afraid rather than insecure but isn't that natural when you find something precious that you don't want to lose as soon as you've found it. I remember buying a book once to read on a long train journey and I started to read it and read it most of the way and it was a super book I got about a third of the way through but when I got off either in a rush or somehow distracted I actually left it behind and so the train carried on without me but with my book and even though I knew I could just buy another copy and carry on reading where I'd left off I couldn't bring myself to do so because I'd invested so much in that one physical copy… Maybe that doesn't make sense. Does it make sense? Eventually when we'd sorted out some of the bulkier mundane things and Anne had decided to move

with her work after which we'd start to live together at that point I
was sure we'd become a proper couple because all the evidence
said that we were and I lost that anxiety that fear of me letting her
slip away it was only then that I felt able to share her properly with
Mum and Dad. She hadn't been pestering me to meet them I think
she was absorbed in the day-to-day the organising the planning she
seemed content with how we were what we were becoming. Yes
she asked questions about them about Matt and Stella but then she
asked questions about lots of things like my job but I never had any
desire to take her into work and show her what I did share her
with my fellow workers my desk the coffee machine. Josh could
have done that if she'd wanted him to and though we saw him
socially a little more because he was her brother after all and doing
so became so much easier when she was living in the same town as
him he pretty much left us alone too and I never felt any
compulsion to change my relationship with him for which I was
very grateful because to be honest I've never been that good at
faking anything.

Josh: Anne never gave me any reason to doubt otherwise, especially
when she moved in with Luke. She'd given me no cause to
challenge the genuineness of their relationship nor the assumption
that they were happy enough. Seeing her more regularly quelled
any fears I may have had - though to be honest it would have been
too late by then anyway. What was that, nearly a year after
Staithes? They never seemed to be in any hurry. In a way it wasn't
a new reality of course, not for her. An altered one perhaps, but not
new. It wasn't as if she'd never had a serious relationship before,
had never tried living with someone. Both Rich and Harry had
been disasters and obviously I hoped she wouldn't suffer in the
same way with Luke. Perhaps the fact they took so long to get their
act together gave me hope, unconsciously I mean. If that was
because it was as much about her being certain as it was about
Luke ceasing to be *un*certain, that was okay with me. You ask
about a new reality; if there was one of those (whatever it might

mean) then it belonged to Luke not Anne - as much as reality can belong to anyone. So they nudged along really, small incremental steps, as if teasing at the boundaries of something; two steps forward, one back, but always edging in the right direction. So what that it took them twice as long as most normal people? Or three times as long? They got there, that was all that mattered. There's a saying isn't there: something about journeys and destinations. When they were finally together, did they regard that as a part of the journey or the arrival at a destination? I have my suspicions. Anne wasn't an arrival kind of person, even if Luke perceived her to be; whereas he - he was entirely an arrival individual. Journeying seemed - to my mind at least - an anathema to him, something to be endured rather than celebrated, a price which had to be paid. If there was one thing I knew about Luke it was that he liked certainty and closure; he hated loose ends and from what I could see they upset him. But then, looking back now, is that really true? I mean, did I really think that at the time or is it just me seeing into the heart of it, now that it's all too late? If I had recognised it at the time, wouldn't I have done something about it, at least had a quiet brotherly word? I try not to think about that too much. The last thing I want to be is complicit.

Stella I

"Tell me about Ambleside, how that fitted in."

I don't know the whole story. Not entirely. You've asked me to tell you everything I can, but this can only be a fragment; the parts which involved me. You might say it's as much my story as anyone else's, though your interest isn't in me, I understand that. But please bear with me. You may have to make an allowance for some bias in my perspective, no matter how disinterested I may try to be. Given what I subsequently felt and what else I now know, isn't it inevitable that my version of events might just be a little - tainted? After all, what value is an initial assessment of someone's character if, after all this time, you know what they ended up doing, what everyone ended up doing - me included - after that long weekend in Ambleside?

I had met Luke a few times by then of course - through Matt, obviously - but I'd never spent any time with him, not real time. Those first meetings had been coloured by what Matt had told me about him, and about how I believed they had grown up together.

No, that's not quite right.

According to Matt they didn't really grow up together, but rather they grew up apart, for a few years just inhabiting approximately the same space. In the beginning - in our beginning - Matt made all the right noises about him to me; after all, what else was a brother supposed to do? But as Matt and I grew closer, he let his guard down, became a little more open about their relationship. And so I was gradually able to see Luke in an unadulterated light.

It's very complicated now, though. Not only because of what Luke did, but because of Matt too. Such events can only change your perspective on people can't they? On life. You look back on them with the blessing of hindsight, and overlay a different reality on them; the reality of the instant is no longer there, corrupted by what followed. 'Then' and 'now', I suppose.

I just want to be clear, that's all.

In the beginning, there seemed nothing remarkable about Luke. Matt and I had been together for a few months. We were nineteen, something like that, trying to fathom out how the world worked: college, studying, being away from home. There were some things he was better at than me, and vice versa. I guess that's why it worked so well, our relationship - the one thing we had to work out together. Luke dropped in on him - on us - occasionally, usually on his way from one place to another; the odd Saturday, or Friday night. It never appeared planned and he never stayed very long. I guess he was taking advantage. Ours was a convenient stopping-off point for wherever he was heading that particular weekend. A sofa for the night; maybe the chance to relive fond memories of his own college days, who knows? He could have had a ball! Being that bit older he had something of an aura about him, imagined or otherwise. I mean the rest of us were all so juvenile, so fresh, and suddenly there was this slightly weird, off-the-wall guy I had some tenuous connection with who was more mature, no longer a student, on his second job, his second car; he'd already lived in more places than I ever had. If you'd have wanted to - and some of my friends did - you could have created a fabric about him, a mythology that turned him into something he never was and never could be. I see all of that now, of course - which was my point a little earlier. If I felt any of it then, any kind of mystique, I can't recall it; if it had been there - and I don't believe it ever was - then it has been expunged from my memory by what I now know.

So his was never a romantic persona. Other than the age difference, there wasn't really anything exceptional about him. He was average I guess. Bright enough, but not obviously so; not good looking, but not ugly either. He was occasionally funny, occasionally generous; but most often he would be aloof, a little distant. One or two of my girl-friends liked that. He could also be mean; once or twice he'd try and put Matt in his place. When he knew he was on solid ground Matt would push back. Their fights - if you can call them that - were strange, wordy, esoteric things. Do I mean esoteric? I think Luke tried to be passionate and angry but never quite managed it. He was always tidy though. He liked things to be ordered and organised. I remember walking into the kitchen one Saturday morning when he'd stayed over for a party or something and he was there at the sink, washing up. He would tidy things away, he couldn't help himself. We even had a private joke: if the house got really messy we'd say we should invite Luke over to get it cleaned up. We never did of course; but we used to laugh about it, about him behind his back. Isn't that what people do? Matt thought it was funny, and I was on his side.

We shouldn't have been at the thing in Ambleside. It was a celebration of some kind - someone's birthday or something. Or perhaps that was just an excuse. There were a few people going and the catalyst was Josh; from what I was told and what I've learned since, those sorts of events seemed to centre around him. Someone's told you all about Salcombe, I suppose? Perhaps it had been Josh's birthday. Anyway it was a big house, slept at least eight if not more, and Josh had arranged the whole thing. There was him, Luke - they worked together - a guy called Chris and his girlfriend (I think she was called Maggie, but I can't be sure), and another one of their work colleagues, Fran, who I think Josh had his eyes on. And then there was Anne. Another couple were supposed to be there too but they pulled out at the last minute. I don't know if it was Josh or Luke's idea to invite us, but Matt got a call; did we fancy a free weekend in the country? Maybe Josh sold the idea, he would have been better at it. Matt had met him once when he went to visit Luke, so it wasn't a totally foreign suggestion. And he was intrigued to finally meet Anne; for some reason, even after so many months, he'd never actually met her. All he had to go on was what Luke had told him, the full rose-tinted version. I don't think he believed him.

So we went. Got the train to Windermere and Luke picked us up from the station and drove us to the house. I remember he seemed unusually chatty; excited almost. It wasn't like him to be voluble. I'd even say 'bubbly', though that's the kind of word which describes him least well. When we arrived at the place I remember whispering to Matt "what's up with him?" He didn't get the chance to answer, but he couldn't really have known could he?

I didn't pay too much attention immediately; Josh was in the throes of sorting out food and drink when we arrived, distracted by showing people around the place, allocating bedrooms, outlining his plans for the weekend at least three times probably. Matt and I got swept up with it all, I suppose. It was a novel experience for us. You need to remember that these people were all older than us. Although no-one was truly very old, to all intents and purposes they were 'adults', out in the big bad world. Even though at that point we'd finished our final year, we still got "University? Been there, done that" a couple of times over the weekend. Anne was half-way to our age though; I mean, half-way between Luke and Josh and us. She offered a bridge in that regard. I remember a kind of magnetism about her, that she could draw you in without you realising it.

"Did you like her?"

Anne? It was difficult not to. Even later, when I obviously wanted to like her much less, it was still difficult. You kid yourself about your feelings sometimes, don't you? I think we all do. So later I tried to pretend that she was evil incarnate - though nothing could be further from the truth.

"Go on."

Bizarrely, there isn't really much to tell, not from my perspective, not about the weekend. It seemed to pass off in the exactly the way you would expect a weekend like that to: we drank a little too much on the Friday night - enough to play Charades! - went for a walk around Ambleside the following morning after we'd had breakfast, then we all went up to Rydal Water and Grasmere in the afternoon. We drank a little too much again on Saturday night, and felt the worse for wear on Sunday morning. There was a suggestion we take the boat down to Bowness - I can't recall who made it - so most people did that, had a walk around Brockhole and coffee there, and then back to the house. People started to pack up and then drifted away. Most people had driven; only Matt and I came up on the train.

"Did Luke drop you back at the station?"

How did you know to ask that question? We assumed he would, but when it was time to leave we couldn't find him. So in the end it was Chris and Maggie who dropped us off. They were heading that way anyway; in fact, they offered to take us considerably further, but we liked taking the train, it was something of a treat...

But it was a strange journey back. We were both quiet, subdued. I was still feeling the effects of too much booze. I assumed it was the same for Matt and that the boat trip hadn't helped. We had to change trains at Lancaster then it was a straight run into the Midlands. We both slept a little on that second leg, trying to catch-up I suppose - though I still didn't feel 100% when we got back home.

"Did you talk about it?"

The weekend? Not much. Inconsequential stuff about Chris and Maggie, about Josh and Fran. We weren't able to work out whether he'd managed to get off with her or not. It was all very strange.

Did we talk about them? Not that I recall. From my perspective there wasn't much to say. Luke had just been Luke; exactly what I'd expected. Tidy, precise. He'd become gradually less voluble as the weekend had gone on - but then hadn't we all? I assumed it was the effect of all that drink. To anyone looking in from the outside, I suspect we would have seemed an entirely different group of people leaving on Sunday compared to those who'd arrived on Friday evening. Obviously we weren't - at least not in the physical sense. Of course, something fundamental *had* shifted, though how was I supposed to know that at the time?

Josh IV

"Tell me about Ambleside, how that fitted in."

I don't think any of us realised it fitted anywhere until much later. But that's in the nature of things, isn't it, our relation to history? It's only when you have the full context, the context applied by the action of events yet to come, that you realise the significance of the past. Can you imagine what life would be like if you could foresee the consequence of your every action just before it happened? Would that paralyse us? Would it change what we did? And always for the better, I wonder? Presumably the world would be a much safer, more harmonious but less exciting place; after all, if you knew bad things would happen because you did A or B, then you wouldn't do them in the first place, would you?

So you ask about Ambleside. Well, if I'd had that kind of foreknowledge then I would never have invited Matt and Stella to make up the numbers. How different might things have turned out then? Oh, you might be one of those fatalist types who would argue that the die was already cast and if it hadn't been Ambleside then it would have been somewhere else at some other time. But I'm not sure I believe that. Aren't specific milestones made up of a unique concoction of smaller events, even nuances, not of what people say but how they say them? Or what they don't say? Take the same group of people - like me, Fran, Chris, Maggie, Luke, Anne, Matt and Stella - and put them in a different situation (the same people mind!) and I doubt you'd get the same outcome. Someone would drink less or more, say or not say something; a look would be shared or it wouldn't. The possibilities are infinite.

Ambleside fitted in because it had to; it could do nothing else. It was woven into the fabric of what became. I don't really subscribe to any fancy theory about cause and effect, or predestination, or any of that shit. It's all random, if you ask me; it's all about luck. Nothing more, nothing less. I don't believe in any 'grand plan' either; if there is one, then what's the point, that's what I'd like to know.

The facts are simple enough. I invited Matt and Stella because we were suddenly two people light and there was a spare room going. Six felt too few. And it was short notice too. I mentioned it to Luke. I can't remember if he suggested Matt and Stella or I did. Because Matt was his brother you might think it was more likely to be him, but I'm not so sure. I'd met them before once or twice. They seemed nice; a bit younger of course, but there was enough of a connection. All I'm saying is that there wasn't any elaborate plan; it was spur of the moment. In fact, I'm not even sure how unanimous the idea was. Did Luke buy-in to it one hundred percent? I suspect not; he never did when it came to Matt. But then again maybe he liked the idea; maybe he thought it was lower risk than a more formal family thing at his parents. I know he'd been fighting that for ages. You'd have to ask him.

But to put it simply, we talked about it, I decided, made the call, they said yes. After was after. But that's how it fitted. Without what came later there would be nothing for Ambleside to fit into.

"You had no inkling?"

As to what might happen? How the hell could I have?!

"But you knew them both, one intimately - after all, she was your sister."

Yes, she was my sister, but that didn't mean I knew the innermost workings of her mind, how she thought and felt! What alarm bells could there have been? Like most people - if not everybody - I was signed up to the notion that she was happy, stable; that things were going well for her. After all, she'd moved house for crying out loud! If anything, it was the opposite: the *not* looking for something, *not* expecting anything. And if you don't look for something, then under most circumstances doesn't that, by default, make you blind or impervious? Or vulnerable? You make assumptions, overlay your own context on events and assume that the combination - those beliefs and what you actually see - are harmonious, aligned. They 'fit' somehow. Was there any point, any point at all, during that entire weekend when I thought differently?

No. That's the wrong question.

Was there any point where I *should* have felt differently? That's the question to ask - and the answer's still 'no'. Emphatically. Was there any point when I *might* have thought otherwise, where I *might* have noticed, been suspicious, made nervous? You choose the words. And the answer then is 'probably' - but only because of now and what has passed. Might I have spotted a glance, a nuance, the way she stood, or said - or not said - something? Of course. But then you could ask the same question of just about everybody there.

"I asked Stella."

You did? I bet she said she saw nothing too - and she'd as much reason as me for spotting something awry. More so probably. But I bet she didn't. She got very drunk very quickly on the Friday night, and I think stayed pretty much that way all weekend. She fell over once when we were playing charades! She was trying to do that scene from "The Karate Kid" when the boy stands on one leg like he's a stork or something. Just fell over! We were in stitches! Watching Matt try and haul her to her feet and then persuade her to go off to bed was almost as funny.

In many respects that was actually a great start to the weekend.

And it didn't really let up. It was only Sunday that things quietened down a little. Everyone was feeling the worse for wear at that point; or at least that seemed the general case. You know when you get to the point where trying to be funny or make a joke is just too much effort and all you want to do is to get through to the end of the day and out the other side? I think that's where most of us were.

"Most?"

Okay. At the time I would have said all of us, but now I know it probably wasn't all, don't I? And yet even when people started to drift away, two-by-two, it all seemed natural enough, harmonious, as it should have been.

If I was quieter it was because things with Fran hadn't quite worked out the way I'd hoped. Not a disaster by any means, but not a roaring success either. You might say 'the jury was out'. As a matter of fact it remained out for a little while, and when a verdict was eventually returned it didn't go in my favour.

But then I go back to my original argument. Had I foreknowledge would I have planned the weekend in the same way, would we have done the same things - would Fran have even been there?

You don't need to answer that.

"And after? What did you hear from Anne?"

Nothing. Or at least nothing out of the ordinary. The same level of interaction, the same conversations, the same tone. When we occasionally saw each other in the pub there was never anything noticeably different, not for what seemed a long while.

And before you ask, it was pretty much the same for Luke. Pretty much - but not quite. There wasn't anything I could have put my finger on at the time, though it's all clear now of course. But then? He was just being Luke - though a bit more so. And as Anne seemed the same, unchanged, I didn't think anything of it. Not once. I know that probably says more about me than them, but at least I haven't tried to disguise it or dissemble. That's the truth, at least as I remember it now.

Luke V

"Tell me about Ambleside, how that fitted in."

I can't believe you've even asked that question given you know perfectly well Ambleside's place in the scheme of things not just in terms of its simple geographical and chronological location but where it sits in the whole web of events. You can't pretend that you don't know or that you haven't asked other people because I bet you have - Josh and Stella people like that - and you will have read about it too even though the language in those accounts would have been more formal and probably harder to decipher but that's irrelevant. My point is you know bloody well where it 'fits in' and so I can only assume you're asking me the question for no motivation other than to torture me to make me relive it to reconstruct and re-experience it and none of that for my benefit.

"I didn't realise what I was doing was supposed to be for your benefit."

Don't get smart with me! You can be as sharp-tongued as you like and weave about with your language to try and deceive me trick me get me to say something I don't want to because it didn't happen or it wasn't true.

"But that's the point. That's exactly what I'm __not__ trying to do. I'm trying to understand the truth, what actually happened. Who else has really tried to get your side of the story - or ever will?"

Only me. Probably.

"You? How?"

The weekend started just fine. Anne had been looking forward to it for some time partly because it was her brother's birthday and partly because we were going to Ambleside and she loved the Lake District and always complained she had never been there enough. Since she'd moved we'd spent more time with Josh socially but because I saw him every day at work there wasn't much attraction for me in more evenings in the pub or doing stuff with him and his various women at the weekends but it was good for Anne to be living in the same place as him again. She tried to make the most of it seeing how close they were not close like twins would be but closer than I'd ever imagined possible between siblings so sometimes they would go to the pub together and leave me out of it which was fine absolutely fine and in some ways a bit of a relief to be honest. There's an irony there of course in that it was her love for her brother and her love for the Lake District that conspired against me and changed things around turned them upside down I suppose for all of us.

Because she was excited about going away for the weekend I was excited too and I remember going to pick Matt and Stella up from the station the two of us having just got back from a quick walk down to the lake - lake Windermere - with barely enough time for me to jump in the car and hare off probably doing the five or so miles into Bowness and the station in record time. It was late afternoon by then you know that in-between time buffering daylight and twilight so the traffic wasn't too bad not as bad as it had been a little bit earlier when we'd driven up trying to get there as early as possible to make sure we could get to stretch our legs before most people arrived because Anne said she wanted to see the water right away and make the most of every minute of the weekend. I cut it so fine that I didn't even have to park in Booths' car park to wait for them I just swung into the station forecourt and there they were standing by their bags having been off the train only a few minutes and it seemed as if it had all been coordinated perfectly. If you were the sort of person who believed in signs you might have taken all that as a good omen for the weekend the fact that we got there in time for a quick walk down to the lake - to throw stones in the water in my case of course! - then to be so on-time in picking up Matt and Stella and when we got back to the cottage we were greeted by the smells of diner cooking and the wine was already open and someone had brought some CDs because they knew there'd be a CD player and Coldplay or someone was smooching through the rooms downstairs. If you'd wanted to make it up it probably would have been just like that with four couples smiling and chatting and buzzing a little everyone ready for a nice evening and a great weekend though in Josh's case he still had his ulterior motive to worry about and so when I talk about 'couples' I can only loosely include him and Fran in that because they weren't and as it turned out were never going to be. As soon as I met her I felt she was too sensible to fall for his trickery and when I told Anne that as an aside at some point in the evening I didn't think she was very impressed with me because I was criticising her brother and even though I told her that wasn't what I meant at all for a few minutes she was a bit quieter and at the time I could only put it down to that.

"At the time?"

I suppose you've heard all the superficial stuff about who did what and when how much we had to drink the walk the following day and the boat ride the day after so you won't be interested in hearing about any of that again I mean what's the point? I'm sure someone talked about charades and Stella's little accident how Josh managed to kick over a bottle of wine the look on his face after he'd done so only matched by an entirely different look when Fran announced she was going to bed and that it was clearly going to be an entirely different bed to the one he was sleeping in - the advantage of having an extra bedroom four 'couples' five bedrooms there should always be an extra bedroom don't you think? But you won't have heard about all the glances that were shared people tending to focus on the clear and obvious the tangible the undeniable because it's easier to feel safe with the indisputable. Stella having too much to drink and falling over because she was drunk when trying to be over-ambitious during a game of charades I mean where's the jeopardy in retelling that given everyone saw it so it cannot be contradicted it doesn't need any interpretation it's the same thing now as it was then so hindsight adds no value takes nothing away. But what about those things that people don't talk about not necessarily because they haven't seen them but because they take an effort to understand brainpower to dissect because it may only be later once you have been able to overlay the events which followed that you can get to the heart of them and the penny drops and you can say "Oh, now I understand".

I'm not saying I understood then and there of course I'm not. If I had been able to do so then things would have inevitably been different wouldn't they so that's not what I'm saying at all but what I *am* saying is that there were things I *did* see and if I didn't understand them in their moment what they meant their significance what they might portend later then that doesn't mean I didn't see them at all does it and if you really want to know where Ambleside 'fits in' then you have to understand those more than anything else.

And before you say anything I know that's what you want that your next question is going to be something about "what did you see?" or "tell me what else happened" or "talk about the things you didn't understand until later"… And wouldn't that last one be a novel in itself not a question or a sentence but an entire book we could all write a book about the things we only understood later that's the story of our whole lives our autobiographies are just that aren't they a series of concrete events that only get meaning later when the next thing in the chain gets applied to them. Well go on then ask away fill your boots because in the same way that you've got no choice but to ask so I have no choice but to answer.

"…"

I should take one of those questions as read then? Or maybe all of them?

It wasn't entirely my comment about Josh's ambitions as far as Fran was concerned that made Anne go quiet maybe it contributed to the moment of friction of misalignment but there was something else too and although it didn't register until later until I'd been able to look back and clear away my default filters only then was I able to recognise it. Because that's what we do isn't it apply filters automatically without thinking because if we didn't we'd be in a constant tailspin trying to process and reprocess everything going deeper into the next layer of meaning and the one after that the backlog growing until we ended up completely mad frustrated unable to strip anything back to its bare bones no matter how hard we tried or the methods we used. The fact was there was something else which silenced her and if I didn't know it then within forty-eight hours I was certain of it no matter how invisible it had been in the first place. If that sounds like a riddle then that's appropriate don't you think? I'm giving you my version of events as they happened to me as best I can without the commentary the gloss the footnotes to try and put you in the same position as I was isn't that what you want some kind of authentic re-telling not just fact fact fact but more of the nuance an unveiling of experience like peeling back an onion? What's the point of giving you the 'now' because you know what the now looks like so you're asking questions because you want to understand the 'then' to allow you to overlay the two together the now on the then to make sense of things. Isn't that what any of us want?

If so we need to talk about Saturday and Sunday.

What happened then? Nothing and everything. If you were looking in from the outside or if the whole day had been recorded as a reality TV show you might have been bored rigid with how mundane the events were no arguments no fights no drama no accidents just a bunch of people relaxing having a good time enjoying a weekend blessed with splendid weather even if it was a little breezier on the Sunday which made the boat ride more challenging for some. On Saturday we strolled into town after a late-ish breakfast browsed in the shops went back for a light lunch lounged about for a while then drove up to White Moss car park at Rydal Water to walk along the west shore up and into Grasmere. Eight people four of each mostly in pairs some at various points holding hands often saying nothing at other times more of a rabble more random as if we kept shaking some unseen dice to decide who would walk the next bit with who conversations more or less animated depending on who you were closest to at the time often the girls together while the boys unable to help themselves stood near the water and threw stones at imaginary targets or tried to out-do each other in terms of distance or how many times we could get a stone to skim across the surface of the water.

"Who won?"

What at? There were lots of subliminal competitions playing out here!

"The stone-throwing."

Oh. Matt. Of course. Even though he was younger than me he was always more athletic stronger agile and so as soon as he could compete at trivial games like chucking stones into the sea or football I was destined to come second and even though I had brute force on my side for a while soon that wasn't enough he became too nimble too fast from that point of view I was used to being beaten by him. At Rydal I had the odd lucky shot or skimmer but it was Chris who pushed him the closest almost throwing as far almost being as accurate but not quite and when we had the girls as our audience he seemed to try especially hard be able to pull out an extra couple of yards to demonstrate his supremacy. The other guys made fun of him of course with him being the youngest there crass comments about youth versus age and how everyone else would excel in things far more important than throwing stones into water but it was only too evident how pleased he was with himself and no matter how hard we tried to belittle his achievements he knew they stood for something and set him apart.

And he wasn't the only one.

"Stella?"

Only at a superficial level the de facto 'that's my boyfriend' pride that's essentially meaningless in my opinion just a cookie-cutter emotion that lets you play to the crowd adopt the poses you are supposed to adopt the sort of thing the reality TV people would have zoomed in on and most people watching would have gone "right, yeah" and simply dismissed it.

"So who should the reality TV people have been focussing on then?"

Isn't it obvious?

Later I realised that my quip to Anne the night before had more or less coincided with a remark Matt had made or a laugh a glance I can't be sure what exactly but there had been something which had provided a counterpoint for my probably puerile joke sufficient for her to regard me differently for an instant. On that walk to Grasmere there was more evidence something less circumstantial and unimagined I couldn't help but notice even though none of the others could because no-one else was attuned to it no-one else watched Anne as much as I did not from any angle to suggest spying or being defensive but because I was still enthralled in thrall and having never shaken that off and being so afflicted what alternative did I have as there were no other options. I was used to watching her benignly benevolently longingly even lovingly if you want and having done so for so long - it was well over a year - I had educated myself come to know every nuance movement expression. There was nothing I could possibly miss. And so when those random dice seemed to pair her and Matt together more than any other combination I began to suspect that the dice might be loaded and not random after all.

But if you asked everyone else or you were able to watch that walk on catch-up TV you wouldn't spot a thing there would be nothing out of the ordinary because you'd see what you expected to see Luke and Anne walking talking holding hands laughing with their friends his work colleague and her brother his brother and his girlfriend and suspect nothing but by the time we reached Grasmere I was a little on edge the sort of on edge which has you hoping that your eyes have betrayed you that you are mistaken and that all he was doing - because I had to blame him - was being nice trying to get to know his brother's girlfriend trying to make the weekend the best he possibly could for everyone. Well bollocks to that!

We spent a little while browsing in the shops the galleries losing each other in the hoards who had come to celebrate what? Wordsworth? I don't think so. It was as if they were ticking off something from a bucket-list and so the place was heaving and it took us ages to find somewhere we could have tea or coffee somewhere large enough to take a party of eight who had just walked in off the street expecting to find a table right there ready and waiting. We ended up at separate tables two lots of four about ten metres apart Anne and I with Josh and Fran he and Anne taking the opportunity for a little sibling catch-up which left me to engage Fran in light and frothy conversation which was never going to happen and we gradually grew quieter Fran because she was struggling with me Josh because he was struggling with her and Anne because I sensed that she wished she was on the other table where they appeared to be having a much better time of things.

"And you? Were you quiet?"

What do you think? I tried not to be but I most likely failed considering what was going through my mind at that point trying to establish whether I was imagining things convinced one minute I was mad and not so the next and even when Anne made an effort to be present on our table and when I made an effort to respond there was something not quite right something missing.

On the return walk I hung back not wanting to be engaged part of it because I wasn't in the mood but also because I wanted to observe from a distance as if I was examining evidence putting a theory to the test. After the walk uphill out of the village and then along the lane before dropping down to the shore again Anne stopped and waited for me to join her holding out her hand in silent greeting forcing me to take it and it was the hand I had come to know and love and I remember looking at it not as if it were an old friend but rather a stranger.

"Are you okay?" she asked giving my hand a squeeze looking concerned and I made some excuse about still feeling a little hungover from the night before even though I hadn't really had that much to drink and she made a comment about me seeming distant - subdued was the word she used - and then we walked together at the back of our little people-snake now spread well apart hand-in-hand nearly all the way as if there was no-one rolling those dice any more. I guess it made a difference I guess by the time we got back to White Moss I felt a little better as if all her hand-holding had squeezed something bad out of me and our quiet chatter - mainly about the others - had proven something of an exorcism and if it's possible to feel better because you've started to doubt yourself then that's where I was even though it sounds like a contradictory argument.

"And Saturday evening?"

More food more drink more games. And later we made love quietly inefficiently and I went to sleep calmed.

I was late up. I'm never late up so it came as a surprise to find myself alone in bed not the first one out to make tea or shower or eat toast and there was a moment of reorientation not only in relation to where I was but how I was. Perhaps unconsciously I replayed the previous twenty-four hours in my head as I struggled out of bed went to the loo wrapped myself in what I used as a travelling dressing gown and made my way to the landing where I heard voices and the clatter and chink of breakfast things. Most people were already down arranged around the table in the big kitchen or standing at the sink posed almost as if they were in a Renoir all freezing mid-sentence mid-movement as I appeared in the doorway all looking my way as if I had caused some great interruption but of course I hadn't not intentionally anyway and there was a laugh or two at my expense and some comments about being a sleepy-head and only then did I realise quite how late it was.

Actually that may not be true. I may have said that because on seeing them I should have realised how late it was their reaction to me ought to have been the trigger for such a response and so I offered it to you just then automatically after the event as it were as if that's what you would have expected of me or I would have expected of myself. But the first thing I noticed was that Anne was sitting next to Matt on the same side of the kitchen table in front of them their mugs too close together for my liking the space between them charged in the way that spaces are charged in paintings and not just by Renoir but others too. Have you noticed how often it's in the gaps between things where the power is and not in the things themselves? Isn't that Japanese? For what seemed an age but could only have been half a second I stared at those two mugs and then it was as if someone unpressed the pause button and things moved on time restarted and I blustered about being late playing along as best I could even though that wasn't my strong suit and Anne reached out to stroke my hand and told me I was an idiot and should go and get showered and dressed and even though she did so in quite a normal natural way I couldn't help getting the feeling she was ushering me out of the room perhaps wanting to remove the space between us the gap where there might have been more than nothing.

I can't remember the shower why should I you might ask it was just a shower after all but that morning everything was more than it would normally have been me crowded on all sides by a menagerie of uncontrollable thoughts. I suppose I was on autopilot and just went through the motions trying to get downstairs as quickly as I could to see if I could re-establish... something. That word you used the other day it was balance or equilibrium yes that was it well perhaps that was why I was keen to get back to the kitchen to see if I could find it or to see what had been lost. But people were already dispersed fragmented: Matt and Stella were out in the garden you could see them through the kitchen window sitting on a wooden bench near the far wall nothing unnatural there Fran was sitting in the lounge on her own reading something she'd pulled from a little bookcase one of those well-thumbed spine-broken novels that people leave behind for other holiday renters I couldn't see Chris and Maggie and then realised they hadn't been in the kitchen earlier so maybe I hadn't been the last one up after all. Josh and Anne were clearing away the breakfast things when I walked in on them a normal domestic scene and I found myself wondering if they would have done that together when they were younger still living at home with their parents their Sunday morning chore perhaps or something they only did when they were feeling especially familial or had been bullied into. Everyone seemed quiet and normal not an emotional hair out of place it felt as if I was the only one who was out of kilter and I began to wonder if I hadn't been mistaken all along but then Josh and Anne stopped talking as soon as I walked in on them the sort of stopping mid-sentence that is an abrupt necessity even though it ends something whose lose threads will be incapable of being picked up right away indeed perhaps not until some time later if at all.

"We're going to take the boat down to Bowness" Anne said explaining they had talked about what we should do with the day immediately I had left the kitchen to go and shower not because I wasn't there but because someone had said "what shall we do this morning?" and that led to a general discussion about what time in the afternoon everyone was planning to leave Matt and Stella's train-time featuring prominently I shouldn't wonder. Then there was a question about the lake the suggestion about Bowness and agreement that if we were on a boat by eleven then we could perhaps even stop off at Brockhole on the way back for a coffee as most people seemed not that enthusiastic to do anything else food-wise. Apparently Stella was feeling rough and not keen on the idea but they'd tried to shame her into agreeing to go though I found myself debating whether Matt might also have preferred her not to and I wondered if that's what they were discussing right now there at the end of the garden he lobbying on behalf of her queasy stomach or throbbing head. At that point Chris and Maggie emerged looking fresher than the rest of us put together and so it was agreed we should get going as soon as we could. Josh banged on the kitchen window to get Matt and Stella's attention then went into the lounge to rouse Fran something I sensed he did with less enthusiasm than he might have twenty-four hours previously.

"Did she go?"

Fran?

"No, Stella."

She did not. Matt made a show of trying to persuade her that she should but it felt a little like a pantomime as if they'd agreed roles while they were in the garden had rehearsed their lines knowing it would look better if he were to be seen batting on behalf of the entire crew. Mind you she did look pretty rough and I suspect the boat trip would have done for her to be honest so from that perspective it was the right call to just stay put but having said that I'm not sure any of us were one-hundred percent except Chris and Maggie who seemed to have bullet-proof constitutions something they'd demonstrated the day before on the walk being the first into

Grasmere and the first back to White Moss beating the rest of us by a street.

We walked down to Waterhead and checked out the various cruise lines that plied their trade on the lake though if we just wanted Bowness and then Brockhole on the way back the choices were more limited one of Red Line cruise ships the extent of its route exactly that. They proved the biggest most popular ships too were well supported and our little group fragmented somewhat as we boarded and then moved about the top deck changing perspectives on the scenery Anne and I close together at the start until Maggie called out something about a place called Wray Castle and Anne moved along the rail to where she was standing pointing at the west shore. I didn't move myself but watched Anne as she leant against the rail the breeze playing in that wonderful hair of hers as if it was being self-indulgent luxuriating feeling my fingers tingling slightly with the muscle memory of how it felt to run them through her hair as the wind was doing now and for a moment it was a kind of reverie until my view was blocked by the appearance of Matt who suddenly planted himself alongside her looking in the same direction pointing too and then saying something which made both Anne and Maggie laugh. Then two strangers appeared at Matt's side to cut me off completely and no matter how hard I tried to see through them it was useless and ended up with me having to avert my gaze when they saw me looking wondering if I was actually staring at them. I turned and leant with my back to the rail trying to appear relaxed nonchalant noticing then for the first time Josh and Fran over the other side of the boat following our progress against the other shore past Langdale Chase and its exclusive bijou boathouse converted to a honeymoon suite something I was sure Josh wouldn't have mentioned to Fran even if he had known about it. Between them there was that distance again small enough but sufficient to be filled with something not quite harmonious and I was forced to think again of Renoir the Japanese the mugs on the breakfast table. Turning back to my right I found the strangers had gone as had Matt and Anne leaving my view of Maggie uninterrupted with Chris now on her other side and I couldn't help but panic at that point wondering where they were if they had gone somewhere to be away from me and even though I located them a few moments later on the other side of the boat heading towards Josh and Fran I think that was the moment that I knew.

"Knew what?"

That something had changed shifted something fundamental had been undone no matter there was no real evidence of anything just then and in spite of that I told myself - or something told me - nothing would be the same again my life was about to unravel not at that moment perhaps but soon enough my anchor was gradually shifting being pulled by an inexorable and undeniable tide and I was going to be cast adrift as adrift as I had been before Anne walked into the pub that day and before she said we should go to Staithes. Perhaps it was thinking of Staithes and that fabric landscape but from somewhere I conjured an image of knitting unravelling remembering my mother's less than professional attempts and I think I must have lost focus for a while because Anne was suddenly there in front of me smiling her hands on my hips and before I knew it planting a soft brief kiss on my lips as if that were the most natural thing in the world to do which only made me feel even more destabilised and if I held her then - as I did - my arms encircling her it wasn't to reciprocate her affection but rather as an attempt to remain upright to prevent a collapse which having crept up on me during the previous day or so now threatened to overwhelm me. But she didn't know that and so laid her head on my shoulder and allowed me to catch the unique fragrance of her hair it blowing about my face the wind still playing with it but now taunting me as if demonstrating what one day soon would be taken away from me forever.

"..."

No smart-arse question? Why am I not surprised?

The rest of the day went by in something of a blur the fog you get when you're not well your head full of cold your mind confused feeling as if you want to be lying down or asleep or anywhere but where you actually are even though you know there isn't anywhere or any activity capable of curing the malaise. So we walked around Bowness for a while me slightly detached struggling with the crowds some of the others going into the sorts of shops I knew they would leave empty-handed not being at all interested in the sort of tat on offer but compelled to go in anyway and when they did I tended to loiter outside standing on the pavement like an untethered but well behaved mutt waiting patiently for its master. Or mistress.

It could only have been a little over an hour later when we made our way back down to the jetty having previously checked out the times of the boats back up to Brockhole and Ambleside and once we were on-board and moving again out onto the water and into the breeze there was a suggestion we bypass Brockhole and go straight to the cottage but I think there was a vote or something and those who wanted to stop for coffee were in the majority so that's what we did. It was packed there too lots of kids running about the park thronging to the tree-tops thing they have and the suspended trampoline stuff and Matt suggested we should all give it a go but thankfully the idea was vetoed and so we went up to the cafe and sat on the terrace overlooking the small formal garden and drank coffee looking down the hill toward the lake. You could ask me who sat next to who or what the conversations were about and I couldn't tell you still being stuck in my fug though I suppose I picked up snippets here and there said little watched others as they walked through the gardens or played on the expanse of park below trying to engross myself in others' lives perhaps not wanting to focus on my own at that precise moment. It was the sort of thing I knew I could get away with because I had a reputation for being quiet distant even a little sullen at times of course I knew what people thought of me they thought it was idiosyncratic that I was a bit of an odd-ball and maybe they were right perhaps that's what history has demonstrated but at that moment in time it served me well allowed me to abstract myself. You might ask me if it was self-defeating and a generally an unattractive trait and whether at that particular point in time when I may have needed to be completely the opposite to be seen to fight my corner to be 'competitive' that to withdraw like that might have been interpreted as defeatist giving up and perhaps Matt smiled to himself and thought "I've won". I don't know. I don't know because I've never asked them and anyway isn't that your job?

"My job?"

We finished at the cafe and then went back for the boat and the last leg to Waterhead meandering up the hill once we were there never coming together again as a group because people began to pack up split into couples - except for Josh and Fran of course - and make their own arrangements. I sorted my stuff out straightaway pulled it out of drawers got it from the bathroom and put it in my bag probably the same one I'd used when we had gone to Staithes and then left the house for a walk. There was no way I could face Matt's leaving and the need to say goodbye to be brotherly and Chris and Maggie had already said they'd take him and Stella to the station so there was no way I was actually needed. From what little I saw of her Stella seemed much recovered by staying there and just reading or dozing or whatever had done the trick and I couldn't help but wonder what might have happened had I done the same how things would have turned out both during the day and later for better or worse.

"For richer, for poorer."

That's a shit joke and you know it.

"I apologise... What was the journey back home like?"

Uneventful. Normal. When I got back to the cottage Matt Stella Chris and Maggie had all left and I was given a bit of the third degree about missing them going so I made an excuse about mistaking the time which I'm pretty sure no-one believed but when I set-to helping sort out the kitchen getting what was left-over of our food together washing up anything that was still dirty they left me alone presumably their gratitude for me doing the chores outweighing everything else.

The drive home? After one final check to make sure nothing had been forgotten we left the same time as Josh Fran having gone about half an hour before us the sort of departure that made it clear that we wouldn't be seeing her again even if Josh was clinging to fading hopes that he could resurrect something. It was one of the things I remember Anne and I talking about as we headed back down the M6 first Josh and Fran and then Josh and girls more generally. She seemed more critical than I'd ever heard her making observations about his approach style call it what you will saying that it was clear to her that he didn't really understand how women worked even after all this time suggesting that he'd blown his chances on the first evening even calling out a couple of examples where he'd made fundamental mistakes 'schoolboy errors' she called them which I thought was pretty damning considering. Remembering how she had reacted to my own quip on Friday evening I kept my counsel only venturing an opinion when it was clear I had no alternative. She talked a little about Maggie and Chris and then about Stella focussing on how much she'd had to drink and her needing to stay behind for the boat trip. It was interesting how critical she was about Stella too feeling she had not only let Matt down but the rest of us as well and although from my perspective it hadn't seemed to have made any difference to Matt - quite the opposite in fact! - I kept quiet there too fearing I might find myself in quicksand and before I knew it up to my neck and unable to get out.

I say that as a joke but that was how I was already feeling sensing the mud oozing around my ankles tugging at me what is it they say that when you're in quicksand that you shouldn't move as movement only gets you dragged in deeper faster. So metaphorically I did everything I could to remain motionless saying little expressing no contentious opinion nor highlighting any observation which might have been open to challenge or misinterpretation. Already quiet such a defensive posture only made me seem more so I guess and after about an hour Anne asked me if I was alright if I'd enjoyed the weekend whether there was anything wrong. I couldn't say partly because I couldn't partly because I didn't know and partly because if I *did* know or thought I knew then how was I supposed to find the words to articulate any of that in a way that was going to be accurate acceptable and not have the quicksand suddenly up to my knees? And I guess that there was a sliver of me that hoped I might yet have been mistaken my reading of the entire weekend flawed from start to finish a part of me that hadn't yet given up that wanted to return to the normality of our day-to-day life and see if what I thought I'd lost or had stolen during the previous forty-eight hours was actually still there just beneath the surface and all it needed as to be coaxed back into the light. Was there yet a rope I could pull on to haul myself out of the mire that seemed to have been created about me?

Things fall apart

Perhaps life is full of moments like that, tipping points. Or then again perhaps every single moment has the potential to be one. And if it does, what elevates it to such importance? The obvious candidates are easy to recognise: the accident or major incident, the windfall, the big decision. But the smaller and more subtle? The moments that are defined by a word, a simple action, no more than whisper? Are they rewarded with their inheritance much later when they can be gilded with context, and when their place in the broader scheme of things can be recognised? Are they promoted via such enlightenment and flagged by exclamations of "ah, now I see!"? Are they created in hindsight, the product of standard deviation between 'now' and 'then'?

Does it even matter? Aren't we merely debating the point at which recognition dawns, rather than the real, tangible and strangely physical moment to which it is attached? And what if recognition never comes at all? What if Luke had missed those subtleties during the weekend in Ambleside; would it have made any difference to what followed?

I think you know the answer to that. Doesn't everyone?

Ask them…

"So things were different?"

Luke: Aren't they always?

Josh: I knew they were going to be, even before we left Ambleside. I'm not blind, and I knew my sister well enough to sense something was going on even before she spoke to me. It was between the boat and the cottage. She cornered me straight away and made sure we walked back together, apart from the others. There was something about her I hadn't seen for a long while, a couple of years probably, like when she came back from that weekend in Staithes. She was excited; there's no other word. She was bristling with potential - and trying desperately not to show it. I mean, I'd noticed there had been a connection with Matt - the Matt who seemed a different person without Stella around, to be fair. And the Matt who seemed to score in just about every department when compared to his brother. I'd seen it, their connection, but hadn't realised just how significant it was. You know when people just hit it off don't you, and I'd assumed - maybe naïvely - that was what I'd witnessed. Part of me probably thought it was really nice that Anne had got on well with Luke's brother; it would have made things easier, for the future I mean. But of course it didn't; it made the future so much more difficult. So *changed*.

I asked her what she was planning to do, but she didn't know. She was still processing it; she acknowledged it was difficult, with both Luke and Stella to consider. "Maybe I won't do anything," she said at one point. "Maybe I'll go home and realise it was nothing at all and we'll just go back to being how we were at five o'clock on Friday." And even though that's what she said, I didn't believe her - and I could tell she didn't believe it herself either.

If I had been worried about how the rest of the day was going to unfold then I needn't have. I didn't realise she was such a good actress! It helped that Luke decided to absent himself when he did, and Matt performed all the duties you would have expected in terms of making sure Stella was okay, doing the heavy-lifting in readiness for their departure. I saw him glance towards Anne once or twice - I was alive to all that now! - but they were looks never acknowledged, no secret messages were passed. When Luke eventually reappeared we gave him a hard time for not seeing off his brother, then left him to tidy up the kitchen, as we knew he would. Once Fran had gone too, the three of us finished off the cleaning and the packing, then headed home. And though I never really found out what the immediate aftermath had been for Matt and Stella, it was the non-dramatic leaving you might have predicted two days previously - including the early departure of Fran, if I'm honest - and so no-one looking in from outside would have been any the wiser. Well apart from Anne and I.

And Luke, you may well ask? Even though I'd known him for a while now - what three years? - he was still difficult to read most of the time. I wasn't fazed by the way his weekend concluded, seeing him quieter at the end than he had been Friday night; after all, social events like that didn't play to his strong suit, and he was probably pissed off with the lot of us by the Sunday afternoon. So his being distant - and he *was* distant - could have been either normal or a sign that he wasn't blind either. I hoped for his sake it was the former.

Stella: Not immediately, but pretty soon after. I didn't really feel myself for a day or so; going back to work on the Monday was surprisingly hard! Matt and I had a tradition that on some Wednesday nights we would go for a curry. At least once a month. There was a small place near where we lived - walking distance - that didn't look very inspiring inside or out, but the food was tremendous. We'd been going there for, I don't know, at least a year. We'd agreed on the way up to Ambleside that we'd have a curry the following Wednesday and when I mentioned it to him when we got back from work he was unusually reluctant. More often than not I was the one who was less keen, so I was naturally surprised. He took some persuading but in the end we went. The place was typically quiet and we were able to get our favourite table, tucked in a corner at the front by the window; great for watching people go by outside, especially in the summer...

Anyway, he was normally reasonably animated; you know, chatting to the staff, debating with them what he should have to eat even though it always seemed to come down to a choice of the same four or five things. They used to play along with him; it was one of the touches that made an evening there so pleasant. But that evening he just ordered; there was no banter. Not only that, there wasn't much of anything: not much talking, no joking, he even struggled to look at me. You know I didn't notice that part straightaway; it was only after half an hour or more that I realised whenever I looked at him his gaze was always somewhere else. He couldn't deny being distracted, so made up some story about his work. There had been rumours for some time about job cuts, redundancies, and he said that he'd heard from someone that the rumours were true, and that any day now they would be deciding who to let go. That was the phrase he used, 'let go'. It's ironic; in a way it sounds like such a positive freeing thing, doesn't it? Anyway that did the trick - partly because it seemed a reasonable excuse for his mood, and partly because it got me thinking about what it would mean for us if he lost his job. Although we were both working, Matt earned the most; we'd struggle on just my salary.

That set the pattern for a short while. He would get in from work, I would ask him if there was any news, and then when there wasn't it meant I had to keep fretting - and keep excusing him for not being himself.

When he started being away more - travelling to work on a project he said - I suggested it was surely good news, evidence that he was important to the business. How could they possibly make him redundant? He said it didn't work like that. And then one day he told me that his father hadn't been well and he was going to pop over and see his parents a little more frequently. Every time he came back from either seeing them or working on that project he seemed down, flat. It all fitted - and I bought it all.

I had no reason not to. We'd been together for over three years; all through University and now living together - working for different companies, but in the same town, living in the same flat. He'd never lied to me - I was convinced of that - and so why should I have doubted any of his stories?

So we muddled on for weeks; a few months. There were some brighter moments, but not many. It was as if someone had extracted something fundamental from him, our relationship. I even began to wonder if it was me, if I had done something wrong. I tried to find a reason, wracked my brain to conjure up a root cause, but I came up with nothing. Obviously I now know if I had taken that Sunday afternoon boat-ride either things would never have changed or I might have had an inkling earlier as to why they did.

Margaret & John: We had no idea.

It wasn't as if they kept us up-to-date with what was going on in their lives anyway, so I don't suppose we should have been surprised.

> It was more like radio-silence than anything else. Neither of them were particularly forthcoming either in what they told us or the regularity with which we spoke to them. They weren't the kind of sons who rang once a week, same day, on the dot.

Neither are we those kinds of people.

> No, of course not. I'm just saying, that's all.

So the infrequent calls became even more infrequent. And when we tried to call them - and when we managed to get through - they we both so…

> Monosyllabic.

I think for a while - a few weeks probably - the person we spoke to most of all was actually Anne, and she always seemed her bright and cheerful self, didn't she?

> Stella less so.

Stella? You never really liked Stella so I'm not surprised she wasn't chatty with you. When did you ever speak to her anyway?

...

But something was up. Maybe we didn't get it straight away, but after a while…

> Matt said it was to do with his work. There'd been all that general financial trouble, stock markets weakening. I knew his sector was under some pressure - manufacturing always is - and so I wasn't surprised; I mean, his story about possible redundancies was entirely plausible.

Perhaps, but my intuition told me it was something else, it really did. And so when he eventually told us that he and Stella had split up, well…

> What we didn't realise was that was only half the story.

Half? Considering what followed maybe a third. Or even less.

> Yes. Maybe less.

Stella: I found out by accident. Well, when I say accident, what triggered me finding out was really just chance.

One day the phone rang. It was a weekend. Having just been out on his bike, Matt was in the shower, so I answered the phone. It was Luke. He seemed - agitated. I tried to find out what he wanted, engage him in conversation, but he said he needed to speak to Matt. I didn't know when they'd last talked - I'm pretty sure it had been quite a while - but given the urgency in his voice it occurred to me that it might be about their father. So I asked him. "How's you Dad?" There was a short silence before he said "My Dad?" I told him Matt had said he hadn't been well and that I hoped nothing was wrong. All he said was "Dad's fine; he's always been fine" - and then he pretty much hung up. I listened to the dial tone coming through the earpiece for a couple of seconds before I put the phone down. I remember it being a strange, hollow, almost mocking sound. It seemed to wipe away all that Matt had told me over the last few weeks, as if it was the manifestation of the vacuum in which I suddenly found myself.

I was sitting waiting on the edge of the bed when Matt appeared from the shower. He asked who had been on the phone. "Your Dad's fine" was what I said; I remember distinctly. And I remember the puzzled look on his face. I told him it had been Luke on the phone and rephrased my previous statement to make it sound as if I had been given good news. As Matt was about to speak I then said "He's always been fine, hasn't he Matt?" Was that cruel? I don't think so. But it gave him nowhere to go. He froze, as if I had painted the floor while he had been in the shower and he now realised he was stuck, unable to move. He was still wrapped in his towel, his hair damp and messy; what had once been an image to provoke desire, now looked vaguely ridiculous.

After his "let me explain" I lost the rest of the conversation - not that there was much of a conversation obviously. He blustered for a short while, trying to explain what he had meant, then why he had used his father as an excuse, and then what he had needed the excuse for. It was so obviously a cock-and-bull story made up on the spot that I let him struggle for a while. He never mentioned Anne once; indeed, he gave no indication that there was any other person involved. It had been an excuse to get some time to himself because he'd taken up a new hobby which was dangerous and he didn't want me worrying, or it was something that needed him to be elsewhere, or he had an old friend who was in trouble and he'd been helping them out... I can't remember exactly, but there was no single consistent, believable excuse. And then I asked him about the time away with work. "Was that real?" I asked him, and he swore it was.

His lying to me was the most painful thing; at least that's what I told myself. Whatever the reason for his deception - and believe it or not right then still hadn't occurred to me that there could be someone else involved - the fact that he had chosen, in a calculated way, to mislead me, to hide something from me, swamped everything else; it meant the trust I had in him simply evaporated. And without that, what was there?

I left him standing there and went and made up the bed in the spare room, then I made a show of collecting the overnight things I needed and moved them out of the bedroom. It should have been him doing all that of course, but I had no idea whether he would or not - nor, if he put up some resistance, some counter-argument, whether I would be strong enough to resist. Only if *I* absented myself could I stay in control and retain the moral high-ground.

The next week was hell. I wanted everything to go back to the way it had been. For a couple of days Matt tried to win me round; I didn't see him that much as we were both busy with work, but when we were together he was pulling out all the stops. If I had believed him to be sincere I might have cracked. And then he stopped trying. And a few days after that I came home from work to find he'd moved most of his things out. There was a note saying he was sorry and that he'd collect everything else when he knew I wouldn't be around.

And suddenly that was that. In what seemed like a flash, over four years evaporated. A month later I found out why.

Josh: Finding out from Anne that Matt had left Stella simply raised the stakes. I guessed they had been seeing each other ever since the Ambleside weekend but I hadn't been able to gauge from her how things were going, how serious it was. It was so out of character! How was Luke? He was the least of my concerns. Matt making a break from Stella nailed his colours to the mast, burned his bridges - or whatever metaphor you might choose to use. I didn't know Stella at all, really, but I guessed she'd never want him back, whatever the circumstances. Why would she?

But now that Matt had played his hand - 'all in', as it were - he was forcing Anne to make a decision of her own. She either had to follow suit, leave Luke and put all her eggs in Matt's basket, or she had to finish with him. Not quite better the devil you know, but you get my drift.

She came to see me a couple of days after Matt had packed his bags. Apparently he was staying with an old friend as a temporary measure until he found something 'more permanent'. What 'more permanent' might look like Anne knew depended on her. That evening we talked through her options - or rather she talked and I listened. I prompted here and there when I thought it appropriate, answered a direct question when I was asked one, but mainly it was her show, laying out various scenarios before me as if I was some kind of lab rat, interested to see how I reacted. Of course she was the only true recipient for her arguments and counter-arguments; I was just the mirror, the sounding board that played them all back to her. She was testing herself; my presence was almost irrelevant.

At the beginning of the evening I honestly believe she was undecided, if anything leaning slightly in Luke's favour; but something made her turn. I don't know what. After about an hour she started praising Luke's qualities, what was great about being with him. And that rang alarm bells. They were the justifications one makes in order to forego them, almost as if she were weighing them on an invisible scale to see how they measured up. Against what, I wasn't sure. It was strange to hear her praising him, sensing the more she did so the further he was slipping away. If Matt had been in the room he would have been rubbing his hands with glee - or relief - knowing she was about to rescue him. Maybe that's what she did, rescue people. After all hadn't she rescued Luke? He hadn't needed rescuing in quite the same way as Matt did at that moment, but he'd needed saving nonetheless. And now she had another hopeless case on her hands - the major complicating factor being they were brothers. Did she register that? You know, I'm not sure she did. I think sometimes she worked at a much more fundamental level; subtlety was worth little when faced with a decision that was essentially black-or-white. And this one was. The middle ground she had been playing for a number of weeks - dangerous middle ground, in a very practical way the antithesis of 'no-man's-land' - had been whipped away from beneath her.

"What are you going to do?" I asked her at the open front door as she pulled on her coat. Even though she said "I don't know", I was sure she did. Whether or not she had chosen to recognise it herself just yet, her mind was made up.

Luke: It was as if I'd gone to Ambleside with one person and come home with another someone who was the same on the outside who did the same things and said the same things who was - on the face of it - as loving and caring as they had been before but underneath they were changed. I don't think I could possibly say if that change was because something had been added or taken away you could argue it both ways I suppose although I never did at the time and only do so now because I am prompted to do so by your questions your interminable questions.

But different? Yes.

How do you put your finger on something like that if you're not permitted to answer as baldly and simply as you'd like? I guess you have to look for evidence the tangible the things that happened or didn't happen that gave context to the 'difference' whatever that might mean and of all those 'different' things how many were truly noticed and registered in 'real time' as opposed to now with me sitting here in my room dredging up my past as if it were a sport? Now and then. Then and now.

She went out a little more stories about new friends at work and social groups she had joined there was a book group apparently and some evenings she'd disappear with a book under her arm and come back after the pubs had closed (they were supposed to meet in a pub the book group I mean) and for sure she started reading more said it was a resolution she had made while we'd been in Ambleside that there were some things she hadn't been doing enough of and wanted to stretch herself though I can't be sure if those were her exact words probably not. And I know what you're thinking that you want to know about our sex life was there more or less of that considering and the answer is about the same which may come as a disappointment to you the same in terms of frequency - though we never went at it like rabbits - but different in terms of intensity duration emotion it was more perfunctory more like going through the motions. I assumed that was all down to her given I was probably not her only sex-partner at that point in time that she was probably getting more of a 'quality service' from a different quarter. Why didn't I say something or act why did I put up with it put myself through it? Well did I know for sure? Perhaps I made assumptions had expectations was looking for a change a shift expecting her to be more reserved less committed but there's a bigger question too isn't there - or another question at least - and that is was *I* any different did that lack of emotion commitment caring stem as much from me as from her because of what I felt and what I had assumed was going on? Oh I wouldn't have thought that at the time of course because the fault - and there was fault in my eyes - was all on her side and so shouldn't everything that was different and wrong stem from her but now looking back did I play my part in our gradual dislocation and I guess the answer has to be yes. That's what time does gives you the opportunity to reexamine the past to overlay the now on the then to reflect on things given reflection is impossible when you're in the moment because the moment is all you have.

And there came a point it may have only been a small number of weeks after we were back from being away that I suddenly realised I was in a sense free that I was no longer enthralled or in thrall yes she still had a hold over me but it was a different hold a more pragmatic practical less spiritual one she had lost that glow her aura she no longer took my breath away. People have told me that's what you do to protect yourself that you find a way to create distance to put up barriers - something I've always been good at! - in order to soften the blow when it comes but don't they also say loss of faith only accelerates the process becomes a self-fulfilling prophecy the downward spiral the free-fall from which there is no escape. If there came a point where you didn't have a parachute knowing the ground was rushing up to meet you and that it would hurt terribly wouldn't you automatically adopt a position where you think the impact will do you the most damage?

If I needed any confirmation it came with that phone call to Matt the one where I'd intended to call him out needing to reach some kind of conclusion or certainty and Stella answered the phone and said Matt was in the shower or something and then she asked that question about Dad and how he was because Matt had told her he hadn't been well and that was when I knew for sure that if Matt was lying to Stella then there was a reason the same reason Anne was lying to me and even though you might argue the evidence was merely circumstantial it was enough for me to convict. I was weighing up the sentence to be meted out when I heard that he'd left Stella and at that point all I could do was brace myself for the crash landing.

Which came less than a week later.

"Was it dramatic?"

Dramatic?! Do you think this was some kind of soap opera being played out in front of millions of viewers a fictitious story being woven by detached and dispassionate screenwriters whose modus operandi was to put their characters through hell just so that they could arrive at a suitable climax week after week all carefully choreographed to not quite conclude just as the boom-boom theme music came to a crescendo. If anything it was the opposite of dramatic opposite because it was expected remember the falling without a parachute thing the being ready and I was ready steeled hardened prepared so that when she came home from one of her 'book club' evenings - without her book, I might add! - and told me of her decision I was protected cocooned and if she expected me to collapse or beg or cry then she was very much mistaken because I had become someone else started to revert to the person I was before she walked into the pub before Salcombe before Staithes. Maybe that made the whole thing easier for both of us I don't know because it felt more like a transaction than anything else an exchange a negotiation carried out more or less civilly. Was that what either of us expected what she expected how can I say? Don't get me wrong there was some anger some tears on her side voices were raised accusations made - and counter-accusations - but everything seemed so antiseptic at least that's how it feels to me now. I suppose my aim stated or otherwise was to escape as unscathed as possible not carry any scars forward remain un-debilitated liberated almost although that's a far too positive a word for what was actually going on.

And so she left. It was an ordered organised well-managed leaving without too much trauma and without drama - dramatic indeed! - although having said as much is that just me saying it now remembering it the way in which I have chosen to remember it providing a gloss an overlay in order to give the impression that throughout it all I was calm and in control? Because I thought I was as I sit here now and try and project myself back - what eight years? - why would I not want to give the impression of me being the detached dispassionate individual totally in control of the situation already over her before she'd even left me before she'd chosen to go off and fuck my fucking brother's brains out.

"..."

I'm sorry. That was uncalled for.

Bristol

And now, suddenly, you are at the nub of things. Although you know you have failed to collect all the evidence - how could you possibly have succeeded in doing that?! - what you have accumulated has led you to this point, in much the same way as the events themselves led the individual participants to their own climax.

For some, however, the drama (that notion so violently rejected by Luke) has already happened. The bit-part players - Claire, Fran, Chris and Maggie - have all come and gone, no more than walk-ons, especially if you consider them from Luke's perspective. They are peripheral figures, colouring-in at the edges, mere tints in the overall landscape. And although there have been other voices, Luke's is dominant, the one you are most interested in; after all, it is his room you have been visiting, and he is the one about whom the narrative revolves. He is at the centre of it all and perhaps in more than one sense this is his story.

Stella's part is pretty much played out too. Although you might regard her as a secondary character, collateral damage almost, she has had something to say; her interpretation of events material because of her attachment to Matt. And whatever you think of her, you cannot deny she suffered, her world torn apart by the actions of others. Was this through no fault of her own? That is a harder question to answer; perspective is everything. How much was Stella a victim? How much might she have been the catalyst for her own downfall? True or false, how is it possible to be definitive? You are inclined, perhaps, to give her the benefit of the doubt, to see her shaded in a tragic light; doing so better fits your overall interpretation, is more aligned to the gloss, the commentary on the central narrative. How can you fail to be sympathetic towards someone who has had their life turned upside-down, their last few years rendered meaningless? Unless you thought she had it coming, that it was an inevitability. Or you simply don't care.

Although you have no desire to hear from him any more, Josh still had his pain to come. He has, in many respects, been something of a ring-master, the orchestrator of Salcombe and Ambleside, the compere who ushered acts onto the stage and gave them a platform upon which to perform. His own preoccupations were essentially tawdry, unimportant affairs, and fundamentally you couldn't care less whether he had been able to make his relationship with Claire endure a little longer - or even establish a relationship with Fran. That he was Anne's brother is what gives Josh his credibility, his authority to speak; and although much of what he says is wrapped in a veil of self-centred concern, elements of his testimony have some validity. Or is that too harsh? Does that belittle him too much? Is that somewhat negative perspective - should you now hold it - born from the palette of Luke's influence? You might legitimately wonder if everything is coloured by him…

The people who should be the most balanced - though not dispassionate - are John and Margaret. If there are any of the players who ought to be even-handed, offer a view without bias, surely it is they, given their relationship to Luke and Matt is identical. Or is it? Might it not be the case that such perfect balance exists only at a physical, biological, DNA-level? When you listen to them, do you not hear preference, leanings to one of their sons rather than the other? When criticism comes - and it is there - is it not dished out unequally? Ah, you might say, but their opinions are clearly not identical. Indeed. As with any couple there is divergence, favouritism; might you not retrace your steps and sift through their words to understand where balance is threatened? But it is not that easy, for in their own way they are interchangeable; how can you be sure who said what, exactly? And you might want to argue that theirs is the greatest burden - but if you did, is that a statement to which you would add the suffix "so what?"…?

Does it all come down to Luke then? Have we reached the point - perhaps as we were destined to from the very start - where we need to hear the remainder of the story from his perspective. Doing so would be a concession, ceding the fact that the narrative is his and his alone, and that the only way we can possibly conclude is the same way we started: with his voice. Of all the players, his perspective is inevitably unique, his influence on events the most direct. You might argue that to this point he has been on the receiving end, the recipient, the acted upon; haven't others - most notably Anne - steered his ship, charted his course? Surely he has (to persist with the metaphor) simply tacked with the wind. But after Ambleside he was forced once again into decision, perhaps the first significant one he had made for some time, one where he - and not others - was at its centre. He talked about going back, reverting "to the person I was before she walked into the pub", and while you can believe that to have been a statement sincerely made, you cannot help but argue that something in him must have changed, the proposition being that no-one can endure what Luke endured - especially that break-up - without some consequence. If Stella was 'collateral damage', is it not possible that Luke was 'primary damage', not in being the target, but rather the individual who took the full force of the impact?

Back in his room you sense something new in the air, a tension, a certain frisson that has not previously been present. Even though nothing is altered (other than the relative depths of the two piles of paper on the table) it feels as if everything is about to be. But how can that be the case? And though you know the story as it was reported third-hand, all that is left is for Luke to tell you - first-person, in his own words - what happened after Anne left him.

"So what happened after Anne left?"

I think I made tea and spent the rest of the weekend cleaning. She chose to leave on a Saturday which made perfect sense practically-speaking and her doing so gave me the chance to undertake something of an exorcism a harsh word implying all sort of things I know but I don't want to call it a 'spring clean' because there was more to it than that. It wasn't just changing and washing the bedclothes and making sure she hadn't left anything behind not just about sorting out the bathroom cabinet or emptying cupboards in the kitchen of the things she had bought which I couldn't stand.

"Such as?"

Tomato ketchup if you must know though I don't really see the significance of redundant foodstuffs do you? I went through the place methodically room by room sorting tidying emptying cleaning and between each room a short rest something to drink to eat taking another bin liner out to the dustbin which luckily had recently been emptied. By the time the weekend was over it was full to bursting and I was spent but satisfied mission accomplished and though you might argue my approach was cold callous that I should have been showing some kind of feeling grief even I had decided not to an arrangement with myself a deal that said if I wanted to grieve then I could do so later at my leisure the most important thing that weekend was to draw a line because without that line there could be no moving on.

And then Monday was work as normal as was Tuesday and the remainder of the week all as routine mundane predictable as I had planned it to be. As you'll inevitably want to know I saw Josh a couple of times from a distance not to talk to and he made no effort to seek me out after all why should he? I had no idea what he had been told Anne might have lied to him too made up some slanderous story about how terribly foul and abusive I'd been and that she was leaving me because of that and not because my baby brother had bigger biceps than I.

"You don't believe that?"

About the biceps?

"No. That Anne would have made something like that up. Not really."

No I don't suppose I do but then there was quite a lot I wouldn't have believed her possible of or others come to that maybe me included and yet look at what happened isn't there a lesson there about who you can trust no-one if not yourself - and then only yourself.

"But that was eight years ago."

So someone's counting..!

"What happened next?"

Nothing happened next. I went to work went home to my exorcised house shopped ate slept returned to my pre-Salcombe routine one week after the next. I had wanted there to be no variation a way to expunge her from my life as if she had never walked into it remember what I said about reverting and so in order to do that I had to turn the clock back and that's what I tried to do. Except I went out much less and I went out with different people after all how could I possibly go out drinking again with Josh not because I was worried my presence might make him feel uncomfortable but because I didn't want him to remind me of her I didn't want to be sitting in a pub with him and see the door open and for the tiniest fragment of a second have some sliver of hope that she might just walk through it so that we could start over try not make the mistakes we presumably had made before.

Crazy really.

Gradually and without me realising it boredom set in. The same pattern as prior years was all well and good for a short period of anaesthetisation to numb the senses but eventually it wore off or wore out or something like that and I realised I was treading water and I didn't want to be doing that. Change and I have never been the most comfortable of bedfellows - had you noticed? - but there comes a time for everything and so I decided it was right to move new town new job not because there were things I was running towards nor running away from either in fact I pretty much wanted exactly what I had at that moment an equilibrium that suited me I just wanted it somewhere else a change of scenery a little fresh stimulation some options for the weekend. I had exhausted where I was. It had been easy enough to clear out the house to scrub surfaces until they were clean and sparkled but you can't do that sort of thing with the bus ride to work or the local supermarket because they don't change and we can't make them change.

"So you chose Bristol."

Not really. I didn't *choose* anywhere. I was quite agnostic as to where I ended up any of the four countries of the UK would have been just fine and any city in any of those four countries it all came down to who offered me the right sort of job and assuming I could make all the practicalities work then it was always going to be a decision made on a first-come-first-served basis. Bristol because it was Bristol no. Bristol because that's where I had the first suitable job offer yes.

"Define 'suitable'."

Really? You really want me to do that?

"..."

Okay. Something I knew I could do that wasn't too menial not too taxing that paid at least as much as I was then earning making any appropriate adjustment for moving to a more expensive town or city a firm that wasn't so small that I couldn't be anonymous nor so large that I could be forgotten about. And the place was important I suppose big enough to have all the appropriate amenities yet close to something interesting lakes the coast hills rivers decent transport links so that I could get in and out relatively easily if I wanted to not too young or too old not too hippy and not too staid. When you think about those as a set of criteria Bristol seemed to fit pretty well as did the firm the job that they wanted to help me with the practicalities of finding somewhere half-decent to live all that sort of thing. All my research suggested the opportunity I'd been offered could tick every box and the fact that it was far enough away from the Midlands was critical because I could never have taken a job in Derby or Leicester as that would have been too much like following Anne too close to Matt too dangerous. I needed some distance and so on reflection perhaps distance was the thing at the top of my list when it came to geographical requirements draw a ring around where I was of about fifty miles or so and anything outside of that circle qualified if I ever wondered whether Bristol was far enough away I can't remember I just know it seemed so and I moved down there settled in and felt safe.

"Safe?"

Yes. Isn't that an acceptable word with all its connotations? Unthreatened comfortable relaxed stable secure out of harm's way a status that fostered balance that allowed me to look forward in a unhurried and unworried way as much as I ever did. I settled into my new job easily enough and managed to find a niche for myself that allowed people to recognise my skills appreciate my contribution without me being a stand-out of any kind it was a role that suited me down to the ground allowed me to be valued trustworthy knowing I was never going to set the world on fire. That's what I became professionally which seemed perfect as it matched the image I had of myself my ambitions for life and though I didn't realise it then and only do so now because of this strenuous interrogation I suppose one of the things Anne had done was to shake me out of that my natural way of being if you like and under those circumstances facing that level of reversal you might well ask whether I was bound to fail at some point because I simply wasn't up to it.

"Isn't that - I don't know - defeatist?"

I'd prefer to think of it as realistic me not looking at myself with rose-tinted glasses and being objective honest clinical almost because don't forget I was the one who had to live with me not you and so I had to be comfortable in my own skin the person I chose to be to create to live with had to be consistent robust reliable.

"And yet…"

'And yet' what?

"And yet that wasn't the way things turned out was it? I mean, you weren't those things - robust, reliable, 'safe' - even though you thought you were."

You're wrong. For nearly six years I *was* those things they *were* me I inhabited them we fitted like hand and glove. I achieved what I set out to achieve.

"But all the time there was something else, something unfinished, lurking beneath the surface. Didn't you feel that?"

Of course I didn't feel that how could I have after all I've just told you! I'd become the person I wanted to be was living the life I wanted to live mapped out planned and scheduled my life ran like clockwork a military machine almost I knew what I was doing every minute of every day I knew what the weekends held for me way in advance I established projects to tackle I took things up like photography and going to classical music concerts not necessarily because I enjoyed them but because I felt I ought to I had succeeded in creating myself afresh anew I was reborn into the

Luke I had sought to be and I felt solid secure impregnable. I even tried dating a little answering the odd lonely hearts ad met three or four nice-enough women but ones who were looking for something that wasn't really me broken damaged women who wanted someone to put them back together willing to take a chance on some man or other to do the job but that wasn't me I wasn't the rescuing kind I wasn't made that way didn't have the capacity or inclination for it. Maybe I was looking for a me in a skirt but I never found one and to be honest I don't think I tried very hard occasionally rewarded with a pleasant evening out a nice dinner and once or twice the beginnings of something usually triggered by a goodnight kiss that opened up the opportunity for much more but which I inevitably closed the door on. Obviously.

"And then one day…"

Don't you mean once upon a time? Doesn't some part of you think that this is a fairy story where the Evil Queen gets the Innocent to take a bite of the apple..?

"If you prefer. 'Once upon a time…'."

Ha! And then one day… I didn't usually go out of the office at lunchtime preferring to work through most of it and cash in with an earlier finish at the end of the day - they had a flexitime system which allowed you to do that - but it had been so warm recently and the office air conditioning was playing up so just about everyone took the opportunity to get outside when then could. I didn't have a set route because I didn't go out of the office regularly normally just to and from the car park or the bus station round the corner and because I always took my lunch in I didn't have to worry about the scramble to M&S or Gregg's or somewhere like that to buy it not that I ate much anyway. I'd been down to the docks and around the Arnolfini a couple of times and once over the bridge and as far up as the Great Eastern though that took a lot out of my flexi-credit so didn't try that again. Once I went into the shops to buy something though I can't remember exactly what so there's no point in asking me.

On the day in question - which as you already know was the 5th of July and as such struck me later as ironic it being the day after independence if you see what I mean - on that day I decided to walk the other way and up towards Whiteladies' Road then back down past the council the cathedral the library returning to the office from there. It was a bit further than ideal meaning I knew it would take me a little longer than I might have chosen to allocate for the purpose of getting some fresh air but I satisfied myself that it wouldn't take as long as the Great Eastern walk and so that made it just about acceptable. From the centre there's a quick way up the hill via a passageway an alley though a bit more than that really a set of steps called 'Christmas Steps' - though don't ask me why - and these lead to Lower Park Row where I planned to turn left past 'The Ship' a venue for one of my speculative dates and then to the end of Whiteladies' down Park Street and back. The steps would be a little bit strenuous but after Lower Park Row most of the walking would be easy downhill and I had no fear of arriving back in the office in one of those unpleasant lathers to which some people so readily succumb and then seem content enough to sit for the next hour stinking out the entire area around their desk. I was fortunate in that I didn't suffer from 'the sweats' like that at least not as much as some other people maybe partly because I never put myself out refrained from anything too strenuous and anyway I had been given a desk slightly set apart from my colleagues so I had a buffer zone around me which gave me some protection from everyone else.

"And vice versa."

I'll ignore that cheap shot you bastard.

"In any case, you're vacillating. Get on with it."

'Christmas Steps'. The name suggests nothing bad should come from using them nothing untoward that they should be positive bountiful more inclined to engender or at least encourage celebration.

I got to the top of the steps and turned left as planned and there no more than twenty paces in front of me walking down the road so away from me which was just as well...Anne and Matt. She had her arm linked through his and was leaning into him slightly they were laughing he obviously having just said something amusing and though I hadn't seen her for all that time I still new it was her even though I could only see part of her face knew it from the shape of her in spite of her wearing a dress I had never seen before knew it from her hair of course which even though she'd had it cut slightly shorter was still as wonderful as ever and for a split second as I froze I swear I could have smelled it. Then someone bumped me from behind on account of my suddenly coming to a halt and I was forced to apologise move forward slightly all of which caused me to lose my focus though I needn't have worried because they were still there a couple of seconds later the after effects of the joke evidently on the wane. Although she looked the same Anne seemed older somehow not just because she evidently was but there was something in the way she walked held herself that suggested she had matured I know that's a bizarre thing to say based on what two or three seconds' impression but she seemed changed in much the same way that Matt had not.

Obviously I had seen him in the intervening period but not that much it was all high-days and holidays so essentially any family event I was unable to get out of those usually dictated by Mum and Dad as they always had been. He had played at being normal with me but in the way someone does when they know they've bettered you got one up when they have a sense of superiority and know such a feeling has pretty solid grounding. Whilst I had tried to avoid him as best I could on such occasions he seemed intent on seeking me out determined to be overtly concerned about my welfare my life what I was doing yet all the time with no other ulterior motive than to rub my nose in it. To her credit Anne always avoided such dos and for a while I assumed it was to protect me but as time passed I came round to the contrary view namely she did it to protect herself.

And suddenly there they were. Knowing it was certain to happen at some point most likely at one of those family affairs I had speculated what I would feel and do the next time I saw them together. But I had never assumed it would be there.

"Then what did you do?"

I followed them.

I let them get another thirty metres or so ahead of me and then set off after them keeping my distance allowing other people to momentarily obscure my view from time-to-time because I knew that would obscure their view too should they on some whim or other decide to spin around if they felt the hairs on the back of their necks tingle get the impression that they were being watched... When they got to the top of Park Street they headed down it exactly the same route I had planned for myself intent on just walking there was no hovering to browse in shop windows something I'd already considered and which I knew would force me to do exactly the same no matter the shop I happened to be passing at the time. I'd given them another twenty yards of so grace as soon as we started downhill toward College Green knowing there was pretty much nowhere else for them to go once they'd reached the foot of the hill other than back towards the centre or off in the general direction of the railway station. As it happened they paused when they got to the Watershed which meant with me now standing at least a hundred yards behind them and still on the other side of the road I had to pause too stopped to watch a sickeningly fond farewell - even after all this time! - for Anne to then head off towards Queen Square leaving Matt to resume after a short pause his solitary walk back towards the centre. I had a choice now as to who I should follow as it was clear to me that I couldn't leave it like that so given Matt was heading in my general direction I chose to follow him crossing roads when it became evident he was heading up Baldwin Street only to lose him moments later as he entered a small office building. Work then.

"You didn't know he was working there?"

I hadn't asked and he hadn't said. And I'd lied to him anyway to them all told them I was living in Swindon.

"And how did you feel?"

If Matt was working in Baldwin Street then it seemed logical to assume that Anne was working in the city too that they had left Nottingham behind and were also pursuing a new life of some kind though as I said I struggled to recollect Matt ever saying anything about moving when we had met at one of those now rare family gatherings but that was probably because I always tried to avoid him and when I couldn't I never listened to him. If those were indeed the circumstances both of them working in Bristol then it was possible such a lunchtime perambulation wasn't a one-off but something of a routine and though it never occurred to me to question why I had never seen them around before - perhaps they had only just moved south - I found myself needing to know if it was indeed a regular thing or whether they were just visiting. So the following lunchtime I made my way up Christmas Steps a little earlier than I had the previous day and stationed myself across the road in a convenient doorway a vantage point which permitted me a decent but discrete view of Lower Park Row along which I assumed they would appear were they to appear at all only to be stunned to see them once again emerge from Christmas Steps. How close had I been to them the previous day?! They could have only been a few feet ahead of me as I turned into the steps myself and surely it was blind luck that had prevented me from running into them then or even on that second day I say luck because the last thing I wanted as to see them bump into them to be forced into an interaction for which I was ill-prepared.

"Ill-prepared?"

In the sense of not having a clue what I would have said to them never mind not wanting to have to say anything at all not wanting to engage be close to listen to speak to them. I had no plan for that.

"So, how did you feel?"

Even though it was less warm the day after that I adopted the same routine getting out from the office earlier still to ensure I protected myself against that unplanned encounter. I had to wait longer this time long enough to force me to be mobile while I waited I mean I couldn't just hang about in the same doorway for fifteen minutes that would have looked weird suspicious wouldn't it but fifteen minutes it was before they stepped out onto Lower Park Row and began their walk to the top of and then down Park Street. I was able to follow from a greater distance this time even walking on the other side of the road something I wouldn't describe as confidence not really but I now knew it didn't matter so much if I were to lose them or if they were indeed to dive into a shop. I confess to have been slightly surprised that they should have adopted such a religious routine it seemed a little out of character for both of them but I guess they had limited time in their lunch break and if they wanted to be together - again, after all this time! - then that would excuse almost anything wouldn't it? And routine it proved to be down to the very spot by the Watershed where they parted and I never once chose to follow Anne because I had my own work to think about needing to get back to the office as rather than harvesting flexi-time I was burning it using up some of the spare I'd built up and I didn't want to get into negative territory. Every day for the rest of that week and all the week after their walk was the same and I suppose because I needed to be sure I got dragged into it and it became my routine as much as it was theirs. We were linked together - invisibly from their perspective - I was joined with them in a way I would never have imagined not that there was any joy in it not at all but perhaps some comfort in that having had them intrude on my life on my routine I had reestablished a modicum of control.

"Yes, alright. But how did you feel?"

You know very how how I felt. You of all people.

At first nothing nothing at all a numbness shocked I suppose thrown discomforted unbalanced all those sorts of things I needed to get my head around get under control because the losing of equilibrium my equilibrium which was the first thing to sort out as without that there was nothing. All I had worked for established honed and whittled away at had suddenly been thrown into disarray as if the ground beneath my feet had turned to quicksand again and I had no confidence about where I could place my feet take my next step. In that sense attaching myself to their daily coming together gave me some of that back a loose anchor in a sense a foundation from which I could rebuild because it felt like I had to redraft the rules of a game that had been changed perhaps that was initially why I followed them every day for the rest of that week in order to hear again the sound of the metronome in my head rather than the vague hissing of silence which had descended upon me. A vacuum. That's what it was.

When the weekend came it was a chance to get back to my normal life to do what I usually did but I found I couldn't commit to the plans already made for the Saturday and Sunday they now seemed worthless what was the point how could I go on as if everything was the same the Bristol I inhabited the place I had moulded to me and moulded myself to was now a different city altogether different because they were in it contaminating it corrupting it. That was the sensation I had early on Saturday morning the sensation that my life could only be different now and it was a sensation which grew and metamorphosed throughout the day and into Sunday and by the end of the weekend it was a hard knot sitting in the pit of my stomach migrated from an ache to a pain from something vague to something hard and unyielding.

As soon as I saw them on Monday lunchtime I knew I had to remove that growth. To operate on myself.

"Yes, yes. But…"

Stop it!

I was in agony. It was as if I was being tortured and on so many levels. Not only had I been robbed yes robbed of my life of how I wanted to live my life not only had they suddenly appeared and destroyed my world they had done it so profoundly that the only way out was for something to change to change going forward or to change by going back. And why should I be the one forced - by them! - to have to change my life again the life I had built up for myself that I was happy living what right did they have to breeze in and disrupt disorganise shatter my existence? None. They had no right at all.

And what made it worse was that it was them.

There were other ways it might have happened this being knocked out of kilter off balance I mean I might have got the sack or been promoted or the company could have been sold my landlord might have refused to renew my contract or I could have been taken majorly ill so all sorts of things might have conspired to displace me because that was how it felt as if I was suddenly alien unwelcome trespassing.

Because of the brother I hated and the woman I had loved.

Have you any idea how trapped that can make you feel those relationships because you can escape neither of them I mean Matt could never not be my brother and I could never not have loved Anne. He was and I did. Alright the first one is factually correct can be proven to be an absolute and the second one cannot because how do you validate an emotion like that you can't it's all subjective and what's more what you think of as love might not be the same as my own definition - though in this instance I think that's one correlation I can be certain of. So it quickly became a question not of how I lived my life but how I escaped from the bars that were suddenly surrounding me confining me preventing me from going about my normal daily business my life. Think about what they had done to me in the space of a week disrupting my routine thwarting my weekend plans they created some unnameable agony inside me made all the more unbearable because on the Sunday night I knew Monday would bring no relief Monday it would all start again or intensify or increase. How could I not follow them on Monday lunchtime or Tuesday how could I let them go on leave them their freedom when they had stolen mine how uneven would that arrangement have been how lop-sided that deal. The prospect was worse than surrender worse than contemplating leaving Bristol and trying to start again because of the spectre they might suddenly turn up somewhere else no matter where I might have been and it was a realisation that I could never be free again not all the time that threat was hanging over me.

Logically the solution was simple. If it was not possible for us to cohabit in the same space the same environs and if I was unable unwilling to change my life my job where I chose to live because of them - and why should I?! - then the only option left was for them to leave to not be there but I knew I simply couldn't walk up to them and say "do you mind going away, far away" why would they and in a way what right did I have to ask that of them that's what they might have said if you were looking at it from their perspective. And if they did leave retreat who was to say that they might not pop up again somewhere else the next time I moved wasn't it likely that I'd be looking over my shoulder forever be on the lookout for them expecting to see them walking in the street ahead of me or bump into them in a supermarket aisle. Over the weekend I had considered the only other alternative which was getting over it making it up with my brother letting bygones be bygones forgive and forget all that trite rubbish but how could I possibly look at him and not think about what he had done to me stolen my life and then reappeared on my patch an itch I could only scratch until I bled. It might have been possible to put Anne behind me if I tried harder at dating if I found someone else it might have been feasible to turn her into a memory an anecdote a story from my past someone I could look back fondly on but none of that was possible because of Matt for how could I look at her and not think of him or look at him and not think of her.

On the Wednesday I waited for them again but not at the top of Christmas Steps nor folded into a doorway on Lower Park Row but in my car in a parking space near College Green a space chosen because it gave me the best view of Park Street one that had forced me to leave work even earlier to ensure I could occupy it using some cock-and-bull story about needing to see the doctor though that was something that proved prophetic soon enough. I sat and watched knowing I was about to resolve my problem that soon I wouldn't have to worry about them any more because I wouldn't have to worry about Matt any more knowing that I would be able to resume my life the life I had chosen and shaped to fit me. And although the plan was simple enough rudimentary even I was certain I could make it look as if I'd lost control I had a ready excuse about someone stepping in front of the car or of a dog running into the road that my foot had slipped from the brake onto the accelerator that I had swerved through the lunchtime crowds as best I could to avoid as many people as possible and if I was clever enough decisive enough credible enough it might even be that I could come out of the whole enterprise a hero a tragic hero who in attempting to avoid a large knot of pedestrians had inadvertently and tragically...

They appeared on cue. I gave them sufficient time to get round the corner and close to the Watershed I knew their timetable well enough to be able to gauge the duration that short segment of their journey took and then I started the car and moved out into the traffic having to force my way out across the bottom of Park Street narrowly avoiding cars heading up the hill because I was working to fine margins a tight schedule and when I turned the corner I saw them Anne just beginning to move away from him Matt pausing as he always did to look at the boats one of the ferries for the museums and just at that moment there was nothing no-one between us and because I was set and could see freedom in my grasp I veered to the right floored the accelerator picking up speed faster than I ever had momentarily exhilarated by that and by the prize dangling before me staring only at him only noticing at the last moment when it was too late that she had heard the car turned to see it ploughing toward him he turning to face me alerted by her shout then then just yards away she began to run back toward him which startled me as that was not part of my plan and in that split second seeing there was no way if I hit him I could miss her I yanked the wheel to the left not knowing if there was time to avoid them to avoid her.

"..."

I regained consciousness as they were cutting me from the wreckage gradually aware of a crowd of people around the car standing a little way back.

My right arm and shoulder hurt more than anything I had ever experienced and there was the metallic taste of blood in my mouth.

A voice was asking me if I was okay wanting me to speak to prove I was conscious. I said something I can't recall what.

Through one of the smashed windows someone in a uniform assured me they would have me out of there in no time out and on the way to hospital. They said as I'd swerved to try and avoid hitting people to try and regain control of the car I'd hit something hard a bollard a kerbstone and the car had rolled. Twice. They said it was a miracle that more people hadn't been involved.

I asked the voice who else had been hurt. Two people the voice said.

"You hit them both."

Although the voice didn't say as much I knew it to be true. I listened expecting to no longer hear the hissing silence of the vacuum. But it was still there when I passed out.

20/20 Vision

You have asked to see his room one last time - and arranged to do so when he isn't there. You want to understand what it feels like to be solitary in the room, in his shoes, and you want to see - with the luxury of time to yourself - whether or not it is exactly as he has previously described.

It is vaguely eerie to be there alone, almost as if, in spite of his absence, he is actually still present, haunting you. But his chair is empty and it takes you no time at all to confirm you are indeed by yourself; after all, where is there for him to hide?

Before you sit down, you pace the room slowly, examining the edges of things, checking drawers for split veneer, the stability of the handles on the wardrobe (though you do not open the doors). For a moment you sit on the bed to gauge whether it is as comfortable as he claimed.

You think nothing has changed. Sitting on the bed you close your eyes and his depiction of it comes back to you, and when you open them again everything is exactly where and how you would expect it to be.

Except for the papers.

During all of your visits his papers have sat in two piles on his desk, and each time there has been some adjustment in them. Looking across to the desk and recalling previous images of the scene in your mind, you now recognise that with each visit one pile grew while the other shrunk. Always the pages were laid face-down, you were never able to see what was written on them, and at no time did he make reference to them. Indeed, more than that, he behaved as if they weren't there at all.

But now there is just a single pile, and although you can tell the sheets are still face-down, they have been moved to within arm's reach of the chair in which he normally sits.

You stand and walk towards the desk, pausing there, allowing your gaze to focus on the sheets and the ghostly shadows of the words written on the other side. From somewhere you suddenly think you hear the caw of a gull and instinctively look toward the window unsure of what you expect to find there.

And then you sit. In his chair. The room has a marginally different perspective from this angle, and even though you know it is the same room with the same furnishings in it, there is something alternate about it.

The pile of papers, when you eventually turn your head towards it, is also different from this angle: it is deeper, thicker than you had first thought. What you had perceived as just a few dozen pages is clearly more than that, at least a hundred-and-forty perhaps; and when you pick them up, still keeping the words face-down, hidden from you, their weight surprises you.

Allowing them to lie heavy in your lap for a moment, you settle in the chair, preparing yourself, as if knowing you are going to be there for a while. Then, with a deliberate breath, you turn the pages over and start reading:

"Hindsight. The most valuable tool we have for making sense of our place in the world. Valuable? How about unreliable, or fickle, or pernicious? Would we be lost without it? We compile histories within the boundaries of our lives as if sifting through the confusion inside a jigsaw puzzle box to find the straight-edged pieces, fumbling them together to make a pattern of sorts…"